OUT OF HIDING . . .

Longarm squeezed off a shot. The Apache's body jerked and he threw up his arms, but stayed in the saddle. Longarm pumped the Winchester's loading lever and slammed it home; now he took quick aim and sent a second rifle slug after the first. This time the Apache sagged and fell from his horse.

With victory almost won, Longarm wasted no time reining his mount straight up the steep slope. No Apaches came out of any of the shelters. Longarm was just beginning to feel relieved that the Indian camp showed no signs of life, when a man burst from one of the shelters. He glanced for only a split-second at Longarm, but before he turned Longarm got a glimpse of his white face and hands.

He'd found his man.

TABOR EVANS

LONGARM

IN THE MEXICAN BADLANDS

JOVE BOOKS, NEW YORK

LONGARM IN THE MEXICAN BADLANDS

A Jove Book / published by arrangement with
the author

PRINTING HISTORY
Jove edition / March 1991

ISBN: 0-515-10526-0

Jove Books are published by The Berkley Publishing Group,
200 Madison Avenue, New York, New York 10016.
The name "JOVE" and the "J" logo
are trademarks belonging to Jove Publications, Inc.

PRINTED IN THE UNITED STATES OF AMERICA

10 9 8 7 6 5 4 3 2 1

LONGARM

IN THE
MEXICAN BADLANDS

Chapter 1

Longarm turned off Eighteenth Street at Larimer and stepped through the always open front entrance door into the always busy lobby of Denver's finest hotel, the Windsor. He zigzagged his way between the clusters of people in the lobby and reached the gambling room at its rear. Stopping just inside the door, he looked around the high-ceilinged chamber as he fished one of his long thin cigars from his pocket and flicked his thumbnail over the head of a match to light it. While puffing the cigar's tip into a coal he studied the busy room.

Even at this early hour of the evening the gambling games in their roped-off area were well patronized. He glanced at the bar, which was visible through a wide arched doorway at the far side of the long room, and saw that refreshment-seekers were packed three deep in front of the gleaming mahogany.

Closer to Longarm, in the gaming room itself, a double row of bettors crowded all three roulette tables. At the chuck-a-whirling, the screen-mesh cylinders on their supporting posts cut arcs through the veil of cigar smoke that hung and swirled above the heads of the players.

An even thicker smoke-veil had collected under the twenty-foot-high ceiling, forming a grayish-white foggy barrier that hid the elaborate frescoes which adorned it. Near the floor the haze was thinner. Longarm had no trouble spotting Billy Vail and his two companions. They were sitting at one of the poker tables behind the fringed velvet ropes that sagged between hip-high brass floor posts and enclosed the faro layouts as well. The big room's four pit bosses moved slowly along the aisles that separated the gaming tables. They flicked their eyes as they moved, looking for signs of cheating or of impending trouble that might disturb the busy scene.

Stepping sideways when necessary to squeeze through the crowded, meandering aisles that wove between the gaming layouts, Longarm made his way to the poker enclosure. He stopped beside the table occupied by Vail and the pair sitting with him.

"It took you long enough to get here," Vail grunted after the exchange of handclasps between Longarm and Frank Allers and Joe Kirby ended.

"Well, I still ain't the last one to show up," Longarm pointed out. He gestured toward the fifth chair, the only one still unoccupied now that he'd settled down. "Where's Ed Crain? Ain't he going to set in with us this evening?"

"That's what I was just asking Frank," Kirby said before either Vail or Allers could speak. "He didn't have anymore idea than Billy or me."

"I can't figure out why Ed hasn't shown up by now." Allers frowned. "While we were closing the office door after we'd knocked off work, I reminded him about our

2

game tonight. He said he'd be here loaded for bear."

Vail nodded. "I'd guess he meant it too. If I recall rightly, we sort of cleaned Ed's plate the last time we played."

"And Ed hasn't forgot that for a minute." Kirby smiled. "He's growled about it damn near every time I've run into him. Last time we talked, a day or so ago, he swore he'd be the one that was going to make the rest of us broke tonight."

"Well, I ain't complaining," Longarm told his friends. "But I'm sorta glad it's him instead of me being the last one to get here. Tell you what. Even if I wasn't last to show up, I'll stand in for Ed and buy the first round."

"Now, I'd say that's right friendly," Allers said.

"It is at that," Kirby agreed. "The game wouldn't seem like it always does if we don't get a little sip to start the evening off, and it won't hurt my feelings a bit if we have one now, while we're waiting for Ed to show up."

"You won't hear me telling you not to," Vail said. "And there's one of those drink-hustling waiters standing by that table over there. I noticed him a minute ago, and it looked like he needed something to do to keep him busy."

Longarm turned in the direction indicated by his chief's nod and raised his arm to summon the waiter. After they'd ordered and the waiter had headed for the bar to get their drinks, Vail fumbled in his inside coat pocket for a moment, brought out a yellow envelope, and held it out to Longarm.

"I guess you can tell easy enough that this didn't come over the government wire," he said. "The boy from the regular office delivered it just before I closed up. You'd

3

already gone, and I figured it might be important, so I brought it along to hand you."

"Now, that was real thoughtful, Billy," Longarm said as he took the envelope. "And I don't reckon it's going to hurt nobody's feelings if I just excuse myself and turn around while I see who it's from."

Without waiting for any of the trio at the table to reply, Longarm turned his back to them and ripped an end off the flimsy yellow envelope. He took out the folded message and glanced at the graceful Spencerian penmanship. "Will get to Denver on the Union Pacific eastbound night flyer," it read. "Hope you can be at the station to meet me. Love, Julia."

Ignoring the curious glances that Billy Vail made no effort to disguise, Longarm refolded the telegram and slid it into the capacious side pocket of his coat. Then he suggested, "If we're going to play any poker tonight, we'd best get started without waiting for Ed to show up. He might not get here for another hour or more."

"I'll go along with that," Joe Kirby commented. "A four-handed game beats not playing, that's for sure. I think Longarm's got the right idea."

"I don't imagine you'd have any objections, Billy?" Allers asked.

"Not a bit," Vail replied quickly. "I'd sooner be playing than sit here jawing. I don't suppose any of us has much to say that we haven't all heard before."

"Then I'll just get one of those floor bosses over here to open us up a deck of cards and we'll get going," Allers went on.

He signaled to the nearest pit boss, who picked up a container of poker chips before stepping up to them.

4

Placing the chips on the table, the pit boss took a fresh deck of cards from his jacket pocket. He displayed the deck before tearing off its wrapper and sliding the cards onto the green baize cloth.

"If you and your friends should need anything more, Marshal Vail," he began, but stopped when Vail spoke.

"Thanks. We'll manage to make out," Vail said.

With a small token bow, the pit boss moved away. Vail shuffled the cards, their small rippling pops attesting to their newness. He squared the deck and spread the cards into an arc on the table's green felt top, then gestured for the others to draw. Allers slid a card from the arc, Longarm drew next, and Kirby chose his card. Vail was the last to draw.

Wordlessly, they flipped the cards face up. Allers had drawn a ten and Longarm a trey. Kirby displayed the jack of hearts. Vail's card was the king of spades.

"It looks like I'm going to deal first," Vail said. "I guess that's my pay for shuffling." He was reaching to pick up the deck when a man stepped away from one of the groups of onlookers nearby and came up to the table.

"I'll apologize to you gents in advance for being so forward," he said. "But it seems to me like you're short a man of what it takes to make a good game. Now, my name's Jim Fields, and I'm a plumb stranger here in town. My friends tell me I'm a middling good poker player, and I sorta like to sit in on a friendly game, one that's not too rich for my pocketbook. If I'm judging rightly, that's the kind of poker you gentlemen play, so I got to wondering if—"

Vail broke in to say, "What you're getting around to saying is that you'd like to sit in with us."

"That's just what I was about to ask you," Fields agreed. "I'd have had to be blind and deaf not to know you're a man short. I like a five-handed poker game myself. Four ain't enough and six is too many, cuts down the number of good hands that a man might expect to hold."

"That's one thing we can sure agree on," Allers said. "I don't guess you're from town here, are you?"

"Just stopping off in Denver until I can catch a train home," Fields replied. "I had to take care of a little business with one of the ranchers up by Greeley, and we got it all wound up before I'd figured we could. The train that'll get me closest to home don't pass through Greeley, so I just decided to save time and took the stage into Denver."

"You're a stockman, then?" Longarm asked.

"I guess you'd call me that," Fields answered. "I've got a little spread over east in Nebraska. It's up on the south fork of the Platte, close to Ogallala. It's not much to brag about, and I'm still right new to ranching, but I figure to learn a lot more. Even the little herd I've got now makes a pretty good living, in case you're wondering can I hold up my end sweetening the pot."

"If you're looking for a big-money game, you won't find it with us," Longarm volunteered. "We're all four hired out to the U.S. government, and you know how stingy old Uncle Sam is with his hired hands."

"Now, I'll tell you, Mr.—" Fields's voice went up on a questioning note as he turned to address Longarm.

"Name's Long, Custis Long," Longarm said before Fields could continue. "That fellow you're standing back of is my boss, Billy Vail's his name. The one by me here

6

is Frank Allers, and the other one is Joe Kirby. Both of them's in the Land Office."

"Well, now, I'm glad to know all you men," Fields told them. "I couldn't help hearing what you were talking about, so if you're waiting for somebody else to show up and give you a five-man game, I'll be glad to cash out when this friend you're looking for gets here. All I'm out to do right now is kill the time I've got to wait before the eastbound night flyer on the UP pulls in."

"That'd be midnight," Longarm said. "We don't play much past that, most times. It just so happens that I'll be meeting that eastbound train myself tonight, so we'll be folding the game up a mite earlier than we might otherwise."

While Fields and Longarm were talking, Vail had been directing questioning looks toward Allers and Kirby. Allers nodded agreement, and Kirby shrugged to show that he was equally open-minded in letting a stranger join them. After bobbing his own head in a nod that he agreed with them, Vail turned back to Longarm and Fields.

"Like you just said," he told the newcomer, "five makes a better game than four. But before we go any further, I guess I'd better tell you a thing or two. We play dealer's choice and table stakes. No round-the-corner straights or made-up hands of that kind. We don't bet the pot shy, but if you run short you can call a sight. Frank, there, generally holds the bank."

"Sounds like we're agreed, then," Fields said. As he spoke, he was taking a wallet from the inside breast pocket of his coat. He went on. "I'm plumb out of hard money, but since all of you work for Uncle Sam, I don't guess you'd turn down his greenbacks."

7

He slid a hundred-dollar banknote from his wallet and dropped the bill on the table in front of Allers, who asked, "You want all that in chips right off?"

"Whatever suits you best. I'll just go along with whatever you men generally do," Fields replied.

"Suppose I give you fifty dollars in chips now and hold the rest back for you to draw out of if you need it," Allers suggested. "If bets get bigger than, oh, ten dollars or so, we usually buy more chips or maybe just toss some real money in the pot."

"Whatever suits you gents suits me," Fields assured him.

While Allers was counting out chips for Fields, Longarm and Vail and Kirby were digging into their pockets for their buy-in money. They produced greenbacks or gold coins: eagles, double eagles, or half eagles. Allers did not need to question them. Acting from long-established habit, he quickly slid thirty dollars in blue, red, and white chips across the green baize tabletop to each of them in turn.

"Whites are a dollar, reds are five, blues are ten," Allers explained to Fields. Then he dug three ten-dollar gold pieces from his pocket and counted out his own supply of chips.

"I reckon it's about time for you to call the game and start dealing, Billy," Longarm observed when Allers had finished sorting the scattered chips and stacking them into neat piles. The other players had already stacked their chips. Turning to Fields, he went on. "You know we play dealer's choice, right?"

"That seems to be the custom everyplace out here in cow country," Fields replied.

While Longarm and Fields were exchanging remarks, Vail had gathered the cards in front of him and was squaring the deck. Now he shuffled twice with quick precise movements and put the deck in front of Kirby to cut.

"We might as well start easy," Vail said. "It'll be five-card stud, first and last card facedown, the other three up. And no wild cards except the joker."

"That makes for a nice honest game," Fields agreed.

Kirby had cut the deck by this time, and Billy Vail started dealing, dropping a card facedown in front of each man and following it with a second, faceup. After putting the deck aside he glanced quickly at the exposed cards in front of each player.

Kirby had gotten the nine of hearts, Fields the ten of clubs. The queen of diamonds rested in front of Allers, Longarm had received the jack of spades, and Vail had dealt himself the diamond king.

Vail put the deck aside while he glanced at the cards in front of each player, then he said, "I guess it's lucky we're all friends. You know me well enough so you won't be thinking I cut my king off the bottom of the deck."

"We trust you, Billy," Kirby said. "Just as long as you don't bet that king too heavy."

"I'll let you off light," Vail promised.

Kirby was already putting a white chip into the pot. "Just out of curiosity, I'll pony up to see the next card."

"If you're willing to pay that much for a nine, I guess I'd better settle for the same dollar on my ten," Fields said, shoving one of his own white chips across the baize tabletop.

9

"If you're putting a cartwheel on a ten, I oughta put in double that for my lady," Allers observed. He was picking up a white chip as he spoke; now he dropped it on the diamond queen that showed on the baize in front of him and added, "But I won't."

"Don't look for me to boost the bet," Longarm said as he added a white chip to the pot. "Not now, anyways."

"Even with this good-looking king, I won't run up the price," Vail told them. He tossed a white chip into the pot and picked up the deck ready to deal the next round. "Things just might change when we see what comes up next round."

While he was still speaking, Vail was dealing another card to each man. On this round Kirby paired his nine, Fields got the diamond six, Allers the six of spades, Longarm the diamond trey, and Vail the seven of hearts.

"She's a pretty lady, but she's not worth more'n a dollar," Allers said, tossing a white chip on the scattering of ante money that lay in the center of the table.

"Well, now, anybody that won't buy one more card, even if a measly chance is all he's got to bet on, is just a piker," Longarm commented, adding another white chip to the pot.

"That's how I feel about the club four I got," Vail agreed, tossing his chip to lie close to the first two.

"And me," Kirby announced as he enriched the pot by another white chip. "My nine's not much better than your four or Longarm's trey."

"I'll stay," Fields announced, tossing in his chip.

On the next deal Kirby's final turn of a card added a diamond ace to the pair of nines already showing. He then studied the other men's new cards. "Looks like my nines are high," he said, tossing a chip into the pot. "Maybe this hand won't be a bust after all."

"I don't drop till the last card's down," Fields commented as he added his chip to the growing pot. "A man never knows what Lady Luck's got waiting."

"And I won't crawfish either," Allers commented as he shoved a chip across the table.

"Seeing as this is the first hand, I'll stay in just to be good company," Longarm observed, following Allers's example in tossing a white chip in the growing pot. "Seeing as how this is just a friendly game."

"I don't guess I can do any less," Vail said, pushing one of his own white chips into the scattering that was growing in the table's center. "Even if the cards I've got now don't give me much to hope for."

"Last card coming," Kirby warned them.

The cards were dealt swiftly, and for a moment silence settled on the table while the players studied the cards they'd received before turning their attention to those dealt to the others.

Longarm's card was the six of hearts, which did nothing to improve a hand that had started with a hidden ten. He made no comment, but gathered the pasteboards into a neat rectangle and pushed it to one side. He lighted a fresh cheroot, then turned his attention to the others.

Vail was also scanning the cards that lay in front of the other players. In spite of the chief marshal's expressionless face Longarm was positive that Vail would be doing as he'd done himself. Even with their hole-cards lying facedown, the cards on the table in front of the remaining players told their own story.

Kirby's hand showed one pair of nines, an ace and a

four. Fields had only a pair of tens, but without making any comment he shoved into the pot the chips required to keep him in the game. Longarm was now sure that Fields's hole card was either a third ten or the six or nine required to give him a second pair. Allers's pair of queens offered the same potential that was in Kirby's spread, either a third queen, or a six or seven that would give him two pairs.

"It's your bet, Frank," Joe Kirby told Allers. "But you'd better have something more than what you're showing now."

"I'll just bet I've got enough to face you down," Allers replied as he tossed two blue chips into the pot. "Let's see you put your money where your mouth is."

"Why, I'll just do that," Kirby told him. Reaching for his chips he picked up two blues and a red chip and dropped them on the scattered array that by now had accumulated in the center of the table. "It'll cost you to find out."

"Not me, it won't," Vail said. He gathered his cards and tapped them into a neat stack that Longarm glimpsed had the same "hidden" ten Longarm's hand had started with.

"I'll boost you, just this once," Fields announced, sliding a pair of white chips into the growing pot.

By this time the chips represented a reasonable amount of money. Allers dropped a red chip on the table atop the whites and Longarm guessed he could be holding a third queen or another six or seven. He raked his cards into a pile and shook his head as he said, "You'll have to settle this one by yourselves. I got sense enough not to throw good money after bad."

12

"That's my feeling, too," Vail said.

"I'll stick," Kirby told them, pushing the necessary chips into the growing pot. "At least for now."

"Let's make it interesting, then," Fields suggested, pushing a blue chip into the pot. "How does ten dollars strike you?"

"Pretty hard," Allers replied. His voice was thoughtful as he went on, adding a blue chip to the pot. "But I don't see any picture cards in that hand of yours. I'll just match your ten."

"Well, I'm going to put another five in," Kirby announced quickly. "If either one of you is bluffing, I aim to find out."

Fields and Allers both met Kirby's raise. Kirby looked questioningly at them, and when both men shook their heads he turned his hole card face up. It was an ace. "Aces and nines beats your sixes and tens," he said. "And—"

"But neither one of you tops my three tens," Fields broke in, turning up his hole card to reveal the ten of hearts.

"Now, I sorta figured that ten might be what kept you in the game," Longarm said. "But I let you play it out, because if there's one thing I can't stomach, it's a damn cardsharp!"

Fields began to raise his arm before Longarm's accusation ended. From the manner in which he brought it up, Longarm realized what the move meant. He drew and fired. The Colt's deep bark overrode the undercurrent from the gambling tables, and the lighter bark of Fields's sleeve gun.

13

Chapter 2

For an instant that seemed to last forever, the thick cloud of yellowish-gray powder smoke from Fields's sleeve gun obscured the card shark. The cloud thinned rapidly, and through the dissipating yellowish haze the other men at the card table could see that the gambler had started to crumple.

Vail had drawn his own Colt only a few seconds later than Longarm. He saw Fields's body jerk as Longarm's slug went home, and kept the revolver leveled. When Fields slumped down to his final sprawl across the chair in which he'd been sitting, the chief marshal eased the pressure of his trigger finger, but kept the Colt in readiness.

Longarm had not lowered his weapon, though he'd known from the moment he fired that his split-second shot was an accurate one. The splintering of wood from the card table's surface as Fields's lead plowed across it gave him a measure of his narrow margin of escape, but his voice was unworried, almost casual, as he spoke to Vail.

"I reckon you can holster up now, Billy," he said. "But I do thank you for being ready to save my bacon if I'd've got off a bad shot."

Longarm did not turn his head away from the body of the dead gambler as he spoke to Vail. In his final crumpling fall, Fields had sagged across the chair in which he'd been sitting, but there was no sign of motion from the card shark's awkwardly sprawled form.

"Why, you'd've done the same for me," Vail replied. "But I've got to admit I can't figure out how you managed to beat that sleeve gun of his with your draw."

"Now Billy, you and me both know that in our line of work there's lots of things a man does even when he don't have time to think about 'em," Longarm replied as he holstered his Colt.

"All I've got to say is that I'm glad I'm in the Land Office instead of on the marshal's force," Allers remarked.

"And I'm real pleased I hold down a desk next to Frank's," Kirby put in quickly. "But you sure played hell with our poker game, Longarm."

Until now, neither Longarm nor Vail nor their companions had become fully aware of the confusion which had been set off by the gunfire. The gaming enclosure had exploded into a babble of motion and loud-voiced conversation. Uniformed bellboys and the clerks from the registration desk were running toward the gaming area. The patrons of the other games were pushing to get closer to the table where Longarm and his companions stood.

Other men and a few women were rushing in from the lobby as the bellboys and porters began trying to form a line that would bar the way to the table where Longarm

16

and his companions stood. After a few minutes of loud and in a few spots nearly riotous disorder, the hotel's attendants began to make headway. As the echoes of gunfire gradually died away, the curiosity of the hotel patrons abated and, at the urging of the hotel's staff members, the patrons began straggling back to their tables or headed for the bar or returned to the lobby.

Longarm and Vail and their poker partners ignored the voices and movements around them. Vail was the first to move. He stepped up to Fields's sprawled motionless form, and when Longarm joined him, the chief marshal was feeling along the gambler's outstretched arm. He began tugging at the dead man's coat sleeve, but the heavy fabric defeated his efforts.

After a moment or two of futile efforts, Vail took out his clasp knife, and while Longarm and Allers and Kirby looked on, he cut the sleeve from its bottom cuff to the cardsharp's elbow. Then he pulled back the fabric and the shirtsleeve beneath to reveal the sleeve gun.

A laced leather casing covered Fields's arm from cuff to elbow. The cut-down barrel of a small-caliber rifle was riveted by short brass brackets to the close-fitting leather sheath. Its muzzle ended an inch or more below Fields's wrist, and an intricate network of finely tooled brass rods at the back of the barrel was fitted with a small circular plate.

"I've only run across one other lash-up of this kind," Vail told his companions. "And it wasn't exactly the same, except that they both take a .22-caliber bullet."

"I only saw two lash-ups like this one before now," Longarm volunteered. "And I never had a chance to give either one of them a good going-over."

17

"It's easy to see how it works," Vail went on. "All that Fields had to do was point his hand at whatever he wanted to shoot at and push his elbow against his ribs. I'd sure like to know who made this for him."

"For all we'll ever know, he might've rigged it up himself," Longarm went on. "But I'll tell you one thing. From now on I'm sure going to look real close at any outlaw that points his finger at me if he's got a coat on."

"It'd be a smart thing to do just that," Allers said.

"Now, I'll go along with that," Kirby agreed. "If I—"

Whatever more Kirby might have intended to say was lost when a man wearing a swallowtail coat came bustling up. He did not introduce himself, but turned at once to Vail and said, "Chief Marshal Vail! I'm very glad to see that neither you nor your companions suffered from this outrage."

"I'm sorry our fracas upset your hotel, Mr. Bush," Vail replied, gesturing toward Fields's body. "But it did get rid of that card shark. He's the one who set off the ruckus."

"You have nothing for which to apologize," the hotel-man said quickly. "Especially since I now intend to impose on you."

"I wouldn't say that anything you asked me and the others to do was imposing," Vail said quickly. "You've gone out of your way to treat me and my men real fine. Just what is it you'd like for us to do?"

"My staff is not accustomed to handling corpses, Marshal Vail," Bush replied. "If I could persuade you and your companions to remove this one to a storage room we have in the rear, it will allow my people to restore order here in this part of the building."

"That won't be a hard job," Vail replied. He turned to his companions. "I don't suppose you and Frank and Joe'd mind doing a little chore like that, would you?"

"Glad to oblige," Longarm replied unhesitatingly. Behind him, Allers and Kirby were nodding their agreement. "If your friend here will show us where he wants us—"

"Just follow me," Bush broke in. "We have storage rooms in the rear where the dead man will be quite safe until arrangements can be made to have him removed."

With the hotelman leading the way, all the poker players carried the dead man to a small storage room at the back of the building. After they'd deposited their sagging clumsy burden, Bush said, "You are the guests of the Windsor for the remainder of the evening, gentlemen. If you wish to finish your interrupted game, please do. If not, the barroom, the dining room, whatever else you wish, are at your disposal."

"I guess all of us can use a sip or two of whiskey," Vail told the hotelman. "But we'll let our poker game go by until another time."

"As you wish," the hotelman agreed. "Just remember that you and your friends are always welcome at the Windsor. Now, there are many small details that I must attend to. If you will follow me back to the lobby, I will excuse myself and go about my business."

Longarm and his companions had tossed off their first drink and were working on the second. Longarm had just touched a match to one of his long thin cigars and puffed it into a glow when he turned to Vail.

"You know, I ain't one to leave good company and

good liquor, Billy," he said. "Especially when the drinks are on the house. The fact is, I got a little personal business to take care of tonight. Soon as I finish off this last swallow, I'm going to bid you men good night and excuse myself."

"Well, all of us can understand that," Vail said. "And I'm not going to stay here very much longer myself. It's been a busy evening, and I need to get to the office early."

"You wouldn't be put out if I was a mite late?" Longarm asked. "It ain't like I was on a case or about to leave on one. Far as I know, all that you need me for right now is little piddling jobs that I don't need to hurry up about doing."

"Yes, you're right about that," Vail agreed. "It's been a long quiet spell, just minor cases and transporting a couple of prisoners to another jurisdiction. Still, I'd like you to get there as soon as possible."

"Sure, Billy," Longarm replied.

Although Longarm had hurried as much as possible when he'd stopped by his boarding house to take a quick bath and put on fresh clothes, he could hear the Union Pacific's midnight flyer whistling the station stop as he stepped into the Denver depot. The passengers who'd been waiting for the flyer to pull in had already gone out to the platform and the depot itself was almost completely deserted. He made quick time by taking long steps, and reached the platform just as the train was coming to a halt.

Knowing Julia's habits, Longarm wasted little time. His long strides took him along the platform to the rear

20

of the train, and he reached Julia Burnside's private car just as it came to a full stop. Julia glimpsed him from the car's front window and waved. Longarm returned the greeting, and was waiting to swing aboard when the porter opened the coach door.

Julia stood in the short narrow passageway that led to the lounge of the luxurious private car. Her arms were already spread to embrace him as Longarm pushed past the porter and took the one long step needed to reach her. Their lips met in a kiss that was not broken until they were forced by breathlessness to step apart. Then they stood for a moment without moving, looking at one another, both of them smiling happily.

"It always seems to me that years have passed instead of months between these times when we can be together," Julia said as she took Longarm's hand and led him into the lounge of the luxurious private car.

"I don't guess I need to tell you that I feel the same way," Longarm replied. "And when you come right down to brass tacks, any time's a long one when we can't get to see each other."

"Perhaps we can make up some of the time we've lost being apart," Julia told him. "I'm staying here in Denver for at least a week on this trip."

"Now, that's the best news I've heard for longer than I can remember," Longarm said. "I reckon you'll be out at your house while you're here?"

"Of course. And I'm hoping that tonight you can come out there with me instead of having to leave on some sort of case."

"I guess we swapped thoughts, even if we weren't together," Longarm said. "Right now there ain't a case in sight that I'll have to be leaving town for. Things are real quiet."

"Then we'll have some time together," Julia said with a sigh of happiness. "And I sent a wire to Caleb to meet me, so we can go home together."

As though her words had been a signal, a tapping sounded at the door of the coach. Then a soft voice called, "Miss Julia? It's me, Caleb. I just got your luggage put in the carriage and whenever you're ready I'll be waiting to take you to the house."

"I won't keep you waiting, Caleb," Julia replied. She turned back to Longarm. "You'll be coming with me, of course."

"It'd take two teams of horses to hold me back," Longarm assured her. "I'm ready to go the minute you are."

During the long ride from Union Station to the imposingly luxurious house on East Colfax Avenue which Julia had inherited from her millionaire father, she had not been out of Longarm's embrace. Now, as they stepped out of the carriage and started into the imposing mansion, Julia turned to him and asked, "Are you hungry, Longarm? Because if you are, I'm sure there'll be a little spread waiting for us. And I remember how much you enjoyed Caleb's wife's cooking the last time we had to be here together."

"Right now, there's only one thing I'm hungry for," Longarm replied. "And I don't guess I need to tell you what that is. Or maybe I oughta say *who* that is."

"If that's flattery, I enjoy it." Julia smiled. "But I'm sure it's the truth, because I've got the same kind of hunger."

22

They moved quickly through the imposing entry to the stairway, and Julia led the way along the thickly carpeted corridor. The instant she closed the door of her second-floor bedroom the restraints imposed on their caresses by the carriage were left behind. The bedroom was large and lighted only dimly by a small satin-shaded oil lamp on a table beside the big double bed.

Julia began dropping her traveling suit to the floor the minute the door latch clicked, and Longarm wasted no time in following her example, but she was the first to be rid of all her garments. When Julia shook off the clinging silk mesh of her pantalettes and the filmy garment slid to the floor, she stepped to Longarm's side.

He was still fumbling with the buttons of his long underwear and Julia said, "Here, Longarm. Let me help you."

"Why, sure, if it'll pleasure you any."

"It does," she assured him. "And helping you undo those stubborn buttons will get us to bed faster."

While Julia bent to unbotton Longarm's fly he was shrugging his shoulders and arms free. Then Julia tugged at the waistline of the tightly fitting trousers until they slipped away.

As the trousers yielded to their joint efforts, Julia saw Longarm's jutting erection outlined under the thin cloth. She left him to undo the final button and slid her hand beneath the fabric to grasp his swollen shaft. She began to squeeze it, and the pulsing of her squeezes speeded up when Longarm bent to caress her warm resilient globes with his lips and the tip of his tongue.

"We're wasting time," Julia whispered as her body began to shudder in response to the continued soft rasping of Longarm's tongue. "The bed's right across the room waiting for us."

"Don't you want to blow out the lamp?"

"No, indeed!" Julia's voice was firm. "I want to watch you share my pleasure. It'll add to my own that we're together again and don't have to worry about time or distance or other people being all around us. Now, take me to bed, Longarm!"

Longarm abandoned his caresses to wrap his muscular arms around Julia's waist and lift her from the floor. He reached the bed in three long strides, and as they moved, Julia freed one arm and slipped her hand between their close-pressed bodies to place him.

When Longarm felt Julia's moist warmth on the swollen tip of his rigid shaft he did not release her, but fell forward when his legs bumped the edge of the waiting bed. Julia gasped, a small muffled cry of pleasure that was smothered in her throat as he completed his lunge and buried himself to a full penetration. Then she locked her legs around his hips and threw her head back to offer him her lips.

Longarm bent forward to find her lips with his, and opened them to match the warm caresses of her entwining tongue. They lay motionless for a few moments. Then as they continued their tongue-caress, Longarm started thrusting. He did not hurry, but held himself to long steady penetrations. Julia's body tensed and her back arched as she met his lunges by bringing her hips up to meet his strokes.

After a few minutes Julia's hips started to rock as she held his kiss, and Longarm continued his slow measured stroking. Each time that he drove into Julia, she

24

tightened her thighs and and pressed down on Longarm's back as though to pull him deeper. Then Julia gasped as she broke their kiss, and a deep throbbing sigh started in her throat.

Before Longarm could slow the steady tempo of his stroking he felt small shudders rippling through Julia's body. She threw her head back, and a rippling chorus of soft moaning sighs trickled from her throat. Longarm read her signs and speeded up the tempo of his stroking. A jerking shudder, then another passed through Julia's quivering frame.

Her sighs became low cries, which mounted for a moment while she writhed and shook and the ripples that were sweeping her body became small, irregular, uncontrolled spasms. Soon Julia's low cries grew in intensity and again she began shaking furiously. Longarm raised his head to glance at her face, and as her lips parted and a low ululating moan burst from her lips, he thrust fiercely with quick pounding strokes.

Julia screamed once, a sharp piercing ululation as she threw her head back and her shaking mounted to a peak of spasmic shudders. Longarm buried himself deeper than he'd thought possible, and held himself deeply within her as her spasms peaked and rippled through her body until she sighed deeply and her quivering form suddenly grew limp.

After a few passive moments had passed, Julia opened her eyes and looked up at Longarm. "I'm sorry that I had to let go instead of waiting for you," she whispered.

"Don't be," Longarm told her, bending to find her lips with his. "I ain't in the least kinda hurry, and I've got enough steam to to last us a while longer."

25

"I'm glad you have." She smiled. Now Julia began working her hips from side to side in slow tentative motions, pushing her pubic arch upward against him as she moved. "Yes, I can tell you have now. Do you want to start again, or wait a while?"

"I'm ready to go on whenever you are, but if you'd rather wait, that's what we'll do."

"I don't want to wait," Julia assured him. Then she proved her readiness by lifting her hips and rolling them invitingly.

Longarm responded at once. He started stroking again, long slow lunges that brought soft ecstatic gasps from Julia. Only a moment or two passed before she began to meet his thrusts with a gentle rocking of her hips.

Longarm paced himself as Julia's fervor increased. He waited until her gentle rocking became violent upheavals, then allowed himself to build, lunging deeper and faster to meet Julia's fast-growing frenzy. The soft moans which had marked the beginning of her first climax began streaming from her throat once more.

Now Longarm started driving harder as he allowed his own climax to begin. When he felt Julia begin to tremble and knew that she was at the stage of losing her control, he let his body take over from his mind. Bit by bit he speeded up the tempo of his thrusts until he was pounding furiously and Julia was crying out with sharp ecstatic gasps.

At last they joined in a quaking, jarring spasm that peaked with a burst of frantic thrusting and heaving. Then their peaks passed and they lay quietly, with no need to speak. No words were needed between them. After a few moments both Longarm and Julia were both sleeping soundly.

Chapter 3

"I'm sorry you've got to report in at your office this morning," Julia sighed. "But I know we can't spend all our time here in bed, as much as we might want to."

"There's a good side to look at," Longarm said. "Billy Vail's told me that all I need to do is show up. I'll be back here with you in two shakes of a lamb's tail."

Longarm was standing only a few feet from the bed, while Julia had not yet gotten up. She was half reclining, half sitting, leaning on a pillow propped against the headboard. Her eyes followed Longarm as he stepped into one of his boots and stomped on the floor to finish driving it on snugly.

"I know you don't have to worry if you're a bit late at the office," she said. "But I can tell that you've been thinking now. I suppose we should've gotten out of bed the minute we were awake."

"If I was running things, it'd take a lot more'n being a mite late reporting to the office to get me out of bed with you," Longarm replied as he reached for the other boot and slid his foot into it. "If I'd've been thinking

27

fast enough last night to ask Billy Vail for the day off when he said there wasn't nothing but run-of-the-mill jobs that anybody could handle, I could've stayed right here and let the office take care of itself."

"That's the nicest compliment anybody's paid me for quite a while." Julia smiled. "You know, Longarm, you and I are pretty much alike in some ways."

"Oh? How can you figure that? You being a woman and me a man?"

"I think it's a matter of being responsible," she replied. She paused to plump her pillow into a more comfortable shape and leaned back against the headboard of the rumpled bed before going on. "I've just been thinking about the little jobs I have to do here. They need some attention. If you were going to be able to stay here all day, I'd feel the same temptation, just to stay here in bed with you."

Longarm had been concentrating on sliding his foot into the other boot, and as he stomped it down as he had the first he said, "I know we've got the same feelings, Julia. But I can't duck going to the office. I'll get back soon as I can, but that'll likely be close to noon. That is, if I'm still welcome."

Julia smiled as she replied, "If you don't get here before lunch is on the table, I'll come to the Federal Building looking for you. Now, kiss me good-bye and get started. And the earlier you come back, the happier I'll be."

When Longarm entered the corridor door and stepped into the outer room of the U. S. Marshal's office, the pink-cheeked clerk at the desk looked up.

28

"Marshal Vail's been looking for you to get here for almost an hour," Henry said.

Longarm replied. "Guess I better go on in right now and tell him I finally got here."

As usual, the door to the chief marshal's office was open. Before Longarm reached it, Vail glanced up from his paper-piled desk and motioned for him to come in. Then he gestured toward the comfortable red-upholstered chair instead of the spindly-legged straight chair.

"I hope you finished up your outside activity last night," Vail said.

Longarm kept his surprise from showing on his face by lighting a cigar as he glanced at Vail across the piles of paperwork that were stacked high on the desk between them. After a moment of silence he said, "I don't perzactly recall mentioning anything to you about what I was going to do last night, Billy."

"You didn't have to," Vail assured him. "Not after I saw the look on your face when you read the telegram I handed you before that cardsharp messed up our poker game."

"Why, hell's bells, Billy, you know I don't try to keep no secrets from you," Longarm protested. "Anyways, a lawman as good as you are can tell what's going through a man's mind most of the time, especially if he knows the man pretty well."

Vail nodded before replying. "I figure that it's pretty hard for men in our trade to keep any secrets from one another after they've worked together as long as the two of us have, Long. And I didn't mean to go breaking in on your private life."

"Why, that don't faze me none, Billy. We've been

29

working together so long that we don't have no secrets to keep from each other."

"Oh, I feel the same way," Vail agreed. "What I was trying to do was—well, to make a sort of apology before I hand you this new case you're going out on."

"I take that to mean I'm going to have to leave Denver for a spell?" Longarm asked. "And you'll look for me to be leaving pretty soon?"

"I'm afraid so," Vail responded. "You know how shorthanded we are right now, with Fredricks still up in Wyoming chasing the bastard who stole that army officer's little girl from Fort Bridger. Slover's down in the south of the district serving warrants. And the new deputy's only been on the job here for three or four weeks. I'd hate to think about sending him out to handle this kind of a case when . . . " Vail stopped short for a moment, then went on. "It's not really a case I'm putting you on, Long. It's more of a job."

"Go ahead and tell me about it, Billy," Longarm suggested. "Whether it's a job or a case, you're the boss."

"You remember Thad Miller?"

"Clell Miller's little brother?"

"That's the one," Vail said. "If you recall, Thad's about three times meaner than Clell was. It's too bad he wasn't along with Clell when his gang was wiped out."

"Oh, I remember Thad, all right," Longarm assured Vail. "Leastways, I remember his name. If you recall, I never set eyes on him. But I ain't forgot him and I ain't likely to. He's the son of a bitch that killed Bob Purcell, and I ain't had too many friends like Bob. From what you told me, he's a real mean piece of work, but you said he's smart too. You mean somebody in our outfit's finally caught up with him?"

Vail nodded. "One of the deputies out of the El Paso office nabbed him a few days ago. I should've heard about it before now, but instead of sending me a telegram as soon as they'd brought him in, the chief down there sent word direct to Washington. I didn't know they'd caught up with Miller until I got this morning's messages on the Attorney General's wire."

"I'd sure be proud to shake the hand of the man that brought in that backshooting son of a bitch," Longarm said. "Bob Purcell was a good friend, and I want to see that Thad Miller buzzard get what's coming to him."

"Well, you'll have a chance to do just that," Vail promised. "I'm sending you to El Paso to bring him back here to stand trial."

"And I expect you want me to leave right away?"

Vail was silent for a moment before replying, then he shook his head and said, "No. I guess they can hold him in El Paso for another two or three days without him escaping again."

"Well, that ought not be too big a job for the chief marshal down there to handle."

Vail was silent for a moment, a small frown forming on his face. Then he said, "I wouldn't put a bet down on that. They've got another acting chief down there since Charley Fusselman was killed."

"Well, I know you've run across a lot of marshals, Billy. Do you happen to know this new chief?"

Vail shook his head as he replied, "Not this one. I'd never heard of him till I saw his name signed to the wire."

"I guess I'd better know his name, if I'm going there."

"I had it in mind to tell you, but—well, to cut it short,

the new chief in El Paso's name is Bass Outlaw."

"Now, stop your joshing, Billy!" Longarm exclaimed. "You don't expect me to believe that!"

"You'd better," Vail said. "Because whether you and me like it or not, that really is his name. It's in the wire I got from Washington."

I guess I've heard everything now," Longarm said, shaking his head. "But if it come from headquarters in Washington, I'd guess it's got to be gospel."

"I'm sure it is," Vail agreed. "But we'd better get down to brass tacks. That fellow Miller is about as slippery as an eel. I don't want to risk him getting away this time, and I don't want you to have to shoot him. I want Miller back here and I want him alive."

"No more than I do, Billy." Longarm said. "And I'll give you my word I'll deliver him thataway."

Vail nodded. "That's good enough for me. Now, with all the work my clerk's got to do, it's likely going to be tomorrow before he'll get around to fixing up the extradition papers and your travel vouchers. And I imagine you'll need some time to get ready. You'll be gone the better part of a week."

"It sounds like to me that you're talking about me getting started day after tomorrow, then," Longarm observed.

"That ought to be soon enough," Vail agreed. "You're not on a case right now, and I don't see any reason for you to be sitting around the office here, getting in the way. I'm sure you've got some off-time coming, so why don't you just take today and tomorrow to look after any personal business you might have."

Longarm was so surprised by Vail's unusual suggestion that for a moment all he could do was to stare at his chief. When he found his voice he said, "Why, that's a real find idea, Billy. I reckon I'll just do like you said. I'll look in tomorrow and pick up the papers and vouchers and get the sunrise train out the next morning."

"I wish we could start right now and have these two days all over again," Julia whispered to Longarm. "You know how much I hate to see you having to leave. But I know it can't be very long now until your train will be getting here."

They'd sought the privacy of her boudoir again after Longarm returned from Vail's office. Julia was snuggled up beside Longarm in the oversized bed. Her head rested on his chest and one hand cradled him at his crotch. On the table beside the bed the night lamp had been turned down so low that only a faint blush of pink came from its elaborate silk shade.

"I don't guess it's likely you'll still be here when I get back, seeing as I'll be away the better part of a week," Longarm said. It was a statement rather than a question.

"Very unlikely," she replied without lifting her head from his chest. "I haven't mentioned it before because I didn't want to spoil out time together."

"Now Julia, you know I understand about your time being short. I know you'd stay longer if you could."

"I could only manage to squeeze three days out of my schedule," she went on. "I spent more time than usual in San Francisco, and I'm a bit disturbed by some of the reports I've been getting from New York."

"You mean somebody that works for you might be making trouble if you ain't there?"

"Oh, no. What I'm afraid of is that the whole country might be on the edge of another money panic," Julia explained. "I was just a child, not old enough to understand what was happening during the panic of '73, but I remember it very well."

"Oh, I can still recall how bad times was. My folks didn't have a lot, just a little hardscrabble farm in West Virginia, but I do know that when I struck out on my own, money was real hard to come by and jobs were few and far between."

Julia said thoughtfully, "What I remember about it was what my father told me when he was teaching me how to handle our family's business affairs. I suppose the most important thing he said was that the quick decisions he was able to make because he was there to take charge saved him from going broke. If something of that sort happens again, I have to be in New York, not Denver."

"Well, I can see why you feel the way you do," Longarm told her. "And talking about have-tos, I have to be on that train early in the morning, so all we can do is not waste what time's left us."

During the last few moments of their pillow chat, Julia's hand had gotten busy, and her caresses brought the response that had never failed her. Longarm bent to kiss her, and without breaking their kiss she rolled on top of him, placing him as she moved. She let the weight of her supple body bring him into her as she rotated her hips and sank down on his rigid shaft until his penetration was completed. Longarm's hands sought the pebbled rosettes of her generous breasts, and Julia leaned forward to allow him to caress them with his lips. Then, except for the impacts of flesh against flesh and

34

an occasional murmured word or two, the room became wrapped in silence.

Since shortly after breakfast Longarm had been looking out of the railroad coach's smudged window. He saw nothing new—the arid semi-desert that had begun when the train left the foothills of the Sandia Mountains stretched away from the tracks, mile after mile to the horizon, without a change. Nothing moved. All that the landscape offered was an unending vista of bare yellowish earth, broken by an occasional low humped sandstone rise and dotted with pale green clumps of spiny cactus.

Leaning back against the worn and dusty green felt of the coach seat, Longarm closed his eyes. He did not sleep, but flicked them open occasionally to take a quick look at the unchanging landscape. The coach was sparsely filled. Only a dozen or so of its seats were occupied. Most of the passengers were men traveling alone, farmers and stockmen distinguishable only by their clothing. The stockmen favored the same Levi's jeans that were worn by the farmers, but while the latter had on blue denim shirts, the stockmen favored short-cut vests over their white shirts.

After what seemed an interminable length of time, the character of the landscape began to change. Barbwire stock fences rose above the ground, and beyond them the dull green of grazing range stretched from them. More often than not the greensward reached the horizon, although now and then a ranch house and its barns and corrals were briefly visible. Between them an occasional unfenced strip of green growth indicated that somewhere beyond the horizon there was a dwelling of some sort.

35

After an hour or so of swaying progress, the train had passed the mixed landscape. Now small houses spaced higgledy-piggledy along a tracery of winding paths were the first indications that El Paso was very near. Then, in the space of a dozen miles or less, the tops of its buildings became visible as they broke the barren skyline.

Within a very short time after the town's outskirts first appeared, the wail of the locomotive's whistle broke the air in a series of rhythmic bleats as the engineer blew the signal that the station stop was just ahead. From his day-coach window Longarm watched the passing scene. A few scattered shanties appeared first, then a narrow belt of residences, and finally the clutter of business buildings that now lined the tracks.

When the first few buildings were passed, the bustle of passengers who were reaching their destination began in earnest. Longarm did not join the stirring. He waited while the detraining passengers lined up at the vestibule, and watched the line grow shorter. When only three or four passengers remained, he stood up, picked up his rifle and necessary bag, and took the half-dozen long strides to the vestibule to reach the steps and leave the coach without waiting.

By the time Longarm stepped off the coach most of the passengers had dispersed. Longarm stopped to touch a match to a fresh cigar before entering the depot. He had not been in El Paso for quite some time, and only one quick glance was needed to tell him that since his last visit changes had taken place.

On his last visit, Fort Bliss had been a small army post. Now it had grown enormously. Behind a stout barbwire fence the orderly rows of the drably utilitarian unpainted

36

walls of the Fort Bliss barracks and stables paralleled the tracks for only a short distance, but away from the tracks the dull yellow walls of barracks and service buildings stretched for miles.

Opposite the fort the rails curved to enclose many more buildings than Longarm could recall having seen in the business section. El Paso had been a town of single-story business houses. Now some of the new structures rose two stories and their eaves were adorned with elaborate curlicues and scrolls of gaudily painted gingerbread ornamentation.

Longarm was still standing near the tracks after the train had pulled out. He was trying to decide which of the new streets that ended at the station he should take to reach the heart of town, and figure out where the Federal Building was located, when a man came out of the depot and walked up to him.

"You'd be Long, the deputy outa the Denver office?" the stranger asked. "The one they call Longarm?"

"Sure am," Longarm replied.

"Name's Ed Connerly," the man went on, extending his hand. "Deputy in the office here. I figured you might need some help finding our new office, so I come to show you the way."

"Oh, I expect I could've managed," Longarm replied. He shook the local deputy's hand as he went on. "But it was right thoughtful of Marshal Outlaw to have you come to meet me, even if I don't rightly need no guide to get to your office."

"You ain't had a chance to hear the news yet," Connerly said. "Everything at the office is still upset."

"Still upset after what, if you don't mind me asking?"

37

"Bass Outlaw's not the marshal anymore. He got killed day before yesterday in a fracas at Tillie Howard's whorehouse."

"You mean he had a gunfight over one of the girls?"

"Nothing like that, Long. Bass was cut down in cold blood while he was just sitting on the sofa talking to Tillie." There was no expression in Connerly's voice. He might as easily have been announcing that it was mid-afternoon.

"You don't say!" Longarm exclaimed. "Did they get the man that shot him?"

"There was two fellows that cut down on him and we've managed to corral both of 'em. Now, both of 'em swears Marshal Outlaw drawed first. I won't call no names nor take no sides," Connerly replied. "You'll just have to make up your own mind."

Longarm did not press for details. He kept the purpose of his visit firmly in mind and said, "Well, it won't be up to me to get mixed up in your office's cases. The only thing I've come here for is to pick up that outlaw named Thad Miller you're holding and take him back to Denver."

"All I can say is, you're welcome to him. He's about the damndest trouble maker I ever run into. The only way we could quiet down the son of a bitch was to tell him that we'd handcuff him to his bunk with a gag in his mouth if he didn't stop his carryings-on."

"I'll do my best to handle him on the way to Denver," Longarm promised. "I want me and him to get on the night train back there, so if we're going to have time to take care of all the pen-pushing we got to do at your office, it'd be right smart of us to get moving."

"Oh, sure," Connerly agreed. "It ain't all that far." He pointed to the barbwire fence that paralleled the railroad track as he went on. "All we got to do is follow the army fence till we get to them tall buildings on Mesa Street. Then we just step along a little ways and we'll be at the Federal Building."

Even before Longarm and Connerly reached the Federal Building they could see that something must have happened in or near it. The street in front of the two-story redstone structure was filled with men. Some of them were gathered in little knots of five or six, talking, gesticulating, pointing toward the building. Others were moving restlessly from one group to another.

"You got any ideas about what's got them fellows all roiled up?" Longarm asked his companion.

"Not right this minute, but we'll find out soon enough," the El Paso deputy answered. He stepped over to one of the men who had broken away from the crowd and was heading in their direction and asked, "You mind telling me what the ruckus up ahead is all about?"

"Why, it seems like one of the outlaws them Federal marshals arrested little while back has got away," the man replied. "I'm in a sorta hurry, so I didn't stay around but a minute. From what I heard, though, the man that give 'em the slip was a bad one. It was that fellow named Thad Miller."

Chapter 4

Neither Longarm nor Connerly spoke for a moment after their informant had hurried on. They stood staring at one another. Though Longarm's expression was unchanged, Connerly's jaw had dropped to set his mouth agape, and his face now bore a worried scowl of disbelief.

"Damn it, Long!" he exclaimed at last. "There just ain't no way for that prisoner to've got out! Why, I was in the office when the night man took over yesterday evening. I heard Doug Harris—he's acting chief marshal, in case I didn't mention it before—I heard him tell the deputy on night duty to watch real close, because he was afraid Miller might start making trouble."

"I'd guess that maybe your night man wasn't listening very good," Longarm commented dryly. "But just standing out here in the street palavering and making guesses ain't going to get us no place. It seems to me like we'll be better off going inside and find out for sure what's been going on."

With Connerly leading the way, they went into the

building. They were greeted by the sound of angry voices echoing in the deserted central corridor. The noise was coming from the half-open door at its end. The wording on the door read *United States Marshal, El Paso District.* Connerly reached the end of the passageway a half step in advance of Longarm. He pushed the door open a bit wider as he stepped across the threshold, and Longarm was only a half step behind him when they entered the big room.

Several paper-strewn desks lined its walls, and chairs were scattered around on the floor to give the office an appearance of disorder. At the far end of the big chamber a half-dozen men were chatting, but as Longarm and Connerly entered, their voices slowly died away. One of the men stepped away from his fellows and moved toward Longarm and Connerly.

"You'd be Long, out of the Denver office," he said, extending his hand. "The one they call Longarm. I'm Doug Harris, and I guess if anybody's in charge here it's me."

"From what I heard, you been having a mite of trouble," Longarm said as they shook hands. "And since it's got to do with that prisoner I was sent to take back to Denver, I'll be real obliged if you'll tell me just what's been going on."

"Anybody who can tell you that is a lot better man than I am," Harris replied. "If you heard anything on the street getting here, I'd guess it's more than I heard. About the only thing I can say for sure is that we've got a dead deputy on our hands and we're short a prisoner."

"That's as much as I heard down on the street," Longarm said. "And it's why I'm wondering what all

42

your deputies're doing milling around here in the office while the prisoner that got away is making tracks."

"Why, these fellows are trying to find anything that'd give us some idea about where he might be headed. But you're right, they ought to be taking out after him." Harris turned away from Longarm and raised his voice. "All right! If you men haven't found anything else by now, that means there's nothing to find! Scatter out, now, and cover the town, and I mean every place from Tillie Howard's fancy whorehouse all the way to crib row! Stay clear of the *barrio* for now. It ain't likely he'll try hiding out in a shanty. Connerly, you take charge of seeing that the job's done right. Now, get moving!"

Within a few minutes the men had departed on their search mission, and Harris pulled chairs for Longarm and himself into a corner of the deserted office.

"Well, Long," the El Paso marshal began. "You sure picked one hell of a bad time to show up, but now that you're here and haven't got a prisoner to take back to Denver, what do you aim to do?"

"I sure ain't going to start back without the man I come here after," Longarm replied. "Even if I got to go out and help your men to find him."

"That Thad Miller's one smart outlaw," Harris frowned. "He's like his daddy was, only meaner. And I guess it's mostly my fault that he got away, even if I don't know all the p's and q's about this job I fell into. I feel real bad about him getting loose, but I feel a lot worse about him killing poor old Shack Ford."

"Now, I already know about your prisoner getting away scot-free," Longarm said. "And from what little else I've gathered since I got off the train, he was the

43

man my chief sent me here to take back to Denver. But it's hard to take about one of your men getting killed."

"What's already been done can't be cured," Harris noted. "Not that it makes our job any easier. But getting down to brass tacks, one of the last things poor old Bass Outlaw did before he got his was to finish fixing up Thad Miller's transfer papers. I ran across them in his desk when I was looking through it, and they're all ready for you to sign. I was just making sure of that when all hell busted loose. Why, we just found that body in the holdover cell less than an hour ago."

"Seems to me like it'd be hard to miss a dead man in a little holdover cell," Longarm observed.

"Not if he was wrapped up in a blanket and shoved under the cot the way he was," Harris said. "If you want to see for yourself, go take a look in the cell."

"Oh, I'll take your word for it that there's a dead man in there," Longarm said quickly. "Just like I'm taking your word for everything else that's happened."

"Maybe you're not coming right out and calling me a liar," Harris said with a frown. "But from the way you're acting, I get the idea that you figure either me or my men have been careless, or not minding our business the way we ought've done."

"That ain't what I had in mind," Longarm replied. "I wasn't saying a thing about your men or how careful they might or might not've been."

"Get on to what you're aiming at, then!" Harris snapped.

Longarm wasted no time in accepting the challenge.

"What I'm real interested in is finding out how you're figuring to catch up with that prisoner I've come here after. How much time you're figuring it'll take to haul him back here so's I can get on with taking him to Denver."

Harris almost shouted his reply. "Damn it, Long, we're doing the best we can! We're not stupid and we're not lazy! Now, I've already sent a man down to the city police station to tell 'em they need to be on the lookout for Miller, in case he's still skulking around town here, and just as soon as I can rustle up enough men from town here and swear 'em in to make a posse, I'm aiming to send some of 'em to Smuggler's Pass and some more down to the Island!"

"Now, hold on just a minute!" Longarm said. "If that Miller fellow knows the lay of the land hereabouts, and I reckon he does, seeing as how El Paso seems to be the place he's been living, you're going about finding him the wrong way."

"Suppose you explain just exactly what you're getting at," Harris said in challenge.

To give himself a quiet moment of thoughtfulness Longarm lighted a cigar. Then he spoke. "This Thad Miller used to spend a lot of time around here before he shifted up to Colorado, didn't he?"

"Well, hell, yes! Him and his daddy before him, they both called El Paso home."

"Now, them other places you named, Smuggler's Pass and that one you called the Island, I take it they're likely to be right close at hand?"

"Sure. Smuggler's Pass is about a half day's ride from town. It's on the old mining trail that runs through some

45

hills a little ways beyond. The Island's downriver a little bit further from here than the pass is."

"You keep calling it the Island," Longarm said. "Do I take that to mean it hasn't got a name?"

"That's what it's always been called," Harris answered. "It's not anything except a pretty good-sized spread of high brushy ground where the Rio Grande widens out and shallows and splits into two branches. There's almost always a bunch of outlaws hiding out there, just like they do around Smuggler's Pass."

"And I guess most of them outlaws comes from our side of the border?" Longarm said.

"I'd say it's about half and half down at the Island, but there's likely to be more crooks from this side of the border than from Mexico."

"Now, let's say for a minute that you're this Miller fellow, and you're running away from a judge that's just waiting to put you in a hangman's noose. Which way'd you go?"

"Why, there's not any question about that!" Harris exclaimed. "I'd head for the Island, and that's for sure!"

"I sorta figured that's what you'd say," Longarm noted. "Because if was I running from a bunch of lawmen I'd cut a shuck for the other side of the Rio Grande, someplace where their badges didn't mean a thing."

"That'd be the Island, all right," Harris agreed.

"And I'd guess a man could spot it pretty easy, even if he was a stranger?"

"Oh, sure. There's not much way anybody traveling in that direction could miss seeing the Island. It's a good-sized spread of land right in the middle of the river. As a matter of fact, it splits the river in two. Parts of it's swampy enough to bog a man down, but there's a lot of good dry land where there's brush and trees enough to give a man on the run a good place to hide in."

"How'd a man expect to feed himself if he holed up there for very long?"

"You know how outlaws do," Harris replied. "The smart ones get their hands on grub one way or another, and there's fish in the river and birds in the air. And I've got a hunch there's a few folks right here in El Paso that make a pretty penny by toting some grub down and selling it."

"Sounds to me like that's the best place to look for this Miller, then," Longarm told him. "Now, I want you to do just what I say, and I'll ask you real polite not to get all stiff-necked and tell me I ain't the one to give you orders because my badge is just the same as yours."

"I'm listening," Harris said. "Go ahead."

Longarm nodded. Then he began. "The first thing I'll ask you to do is send a wire to Billy Vail in Denver. Tell him the gospel truth about it being your holdover that this fellow got away from. Then you tell Billy that I've gone to find Miller and bring him back, and I'll bring him in to Denver soon as I catch up with him."

"I'll do that right away," Harris agreed. "Now let me ask you something. How many of us do you want to go with you?"

"I don't recall saying I was asking for any help," Longarm replied. "Any more'n I'd go out to Fort Bliss and ask 'em to lend me a bunch of their soldiers. You just got one man missing, not no army."

Harris nodded. "Maybe so. But that doesn't change the facts. My men and me know the country and you don't.

47

And what I haven't mentioned yet is that the *rurales* raid that island pretty regular."

"Is that right, now?" Longarm frowned. "How many of their men do they take on a raid like you're talking about?"

"Generally there'll only be three or four. And if our office here gets a case that we've got to work down there, I'll send two. Three at the most."

"And the *rurales* don't bother your deputies?"

"Generally they don't, when there's just one or two of our men going there," Harris replied. "But the bastards that're holed up on it hiding from the law sure as hell do. If we go down there when we're after a real mean fugitive, we'll take as many men as we can scrape up."

"You leave the *rurales* for me to worry about," Longarm advised him. "Just get me a horse and some decent saddle gear."

Harris said nothing for a moment, then he nodded. "I've gone along with you this far, Long. I guess I might as well go the rest of the way. I'll get you the horse."

"And one more thing," Longarm said quickly. "I'll need to make a draw on your office expense money. Fix up a voucher for a hundred dollars or so, and I'll sign it. I'll want all but maybe twenty dollars of it in gold. The rest can be cartwheels."

"Now, wait a minute!" Harris protested. "This is our case, Long! If you figure on going into Mexico and—"

"It ain't up to you to worry about what I'm aiming to do," Longarm replied. "Just write down in your little book that I'm setting out to help you."

"But standing orders say we're not supposed to go into

Mexico unless the high muckety-mucks in Washington gives us permission to cross the border!"

"So they do," Longarm agreed. "But Washington's a hell of a lot further away than this Island we're talking about. And let me set your mind at rest, Harris. I've worked more'n one case along on the border here. I've found out the *rurales* generally don't get stirred up too much about one of us fellows on the marshal's force going into Mexico unless we get too far into their territory."

Harris managed a rueful grin as he replied, "They sure ain't been that nice to us most of the time. But I will say one thing for 'em. They don't get mean as they can be when they run into our men going onto the Island."

"*Rurales* is the last thing I'll be worrying about," Longarm said. "Now, I'll be real obliged if you'll move fast. I ain't had time to get a bite of breakfast or rent me a room here, so just as soon as I get me an egg or two and enough bacon and biscuits to stop my belly from growling, I'll be ready to ride. Except for the grub I need, I don't aim to waste a minute getting started."

"By the time you finish getting your saddle rations and we fix it up for you to get a horse from the Fort Bliss remount station, it's going to be too late to make many miles today," Harris pointed out. "Now, was I in your boots, I'd figure on staying over here in El Paso tonight and striking out at daybreak tomorrow."

"Well, now," Longarm said. "I've heard a lot of folks say that a late start's better'n none, though I never did say it myself. But even if I don't get started before it's close to sundown, I aim to be on the road before it gets too dark to see. So if you'll just tell me the shortest way out to Fort Bliss and who's in charge of the remount station, I'll get on my way and make as much time as I can before it gets too dark to see."

Although the descriptions of the Island he'd gotten in El Paso the day before had been sketchy at best, the instant that Longarm saw the lazily flowing Rio Grande split into a rough Y he realized that he'd reached his goal. In the fork of the Y and a hundred yards or more from the bank, the lighter-hued crests of the rills that broke the river's turgid yellowish meandering current were dividing at the edge of a gently curving shoreline.

Longarm reined in before the horse reached the point of the Y, then toed the animal beyond the split in the Rio Grande and brought it to a halt at the water's edge. Taking out one of his long slim cigars, he lighted it and hooked a knee around the saddlehorn, then sat studying the Island.

As far as he could see through the thick brush that began only a few paces past the point where the stream divided, the Island was deserted. Although the heavy ground growth of hip-high grasses and weeds was thick in the area close to the water, it thinned somewhat where the land sloped upward. Trees dominated the upslope, thin-trunked saplings for the most part, but here and there a bigger tree or two towered above the scrubby ground growth.

Though he could not see bottom through the roiled yellow water, there was the faint ghost of a trail in front of the point where he'd stopped. It led to the river's edge and disappeared below the opaque surface. On the Island's shore at the water's edge, Longarm's close inspection showed the rounded pocks of other old hoofprints, an indication that he'd reached a safe crossing-point.

"Well, old son," Longarm muttered to himself as he studied the trail signs across the narrow strip of water, "looks like you got to where you was headed for. Now all you got to do is find the fellow you're after before he can tuck himself away in a safe hidey-hole."

He toed the horse ahead. When its front hooves splashed into the water, the horse neighed its objection and stomped the soft ground a time or two, but moved ahead again when Longarm prodded it gently with his boot toe. It planted its hooves carefully as it splashed through the shallow water and heaved up the slanting bank until Longarm's tug at the reins brought it to a halt.

On the Island's shore the ground was softer and held hoofprints better. Intermingled with the wavy creases of rainstorms' runoff, there were the prints of a number of horses' hooves. Longarm dropped the reins to let his mount stand, and dismounted to study the pocked ground more closely. At closer range now, he could see not only hoofprints, but the boot prints and sandal prints and occasionally the bare feet of men who'd come to the Island horseless and had waded the river branch on foot.

In spite of his tracking skill, Longarm could distinguish old hoofprints from fresh ones only occasionally; all the prints looked much the same. Even the fresh sharply defined prints of his livery horse where it had come ashore looked neither older nor fresher than half the hoof prints on the narrow strip of shoreline.

"Damned if this ain't as purty a mess as you'd hope

to see in a month of Sundays, old son," Longarm muttered into the quiet air. "Chances are that one set of them hoofprints was left by that Thad Miller, but there ain't no sure way of telling. But there ain't a lot of space to cover, so the only thing to do is keep plugging away at it."

Leading his horse now, Longarm began a methodical zigzagging along the strip of shoreline where he'd emerged from the river. In the soft yielding soil there were more prints than he'd expected to find, both on the Mexican side of the split in the Rio Grande and on the side where he'd just crossed.

Whether they led from the water to the brush or from the thicket to the water, most of the prints were in fairly straight lines. Only an occasional set indicated that a rider or a man on foot had emerged from the dense brush cover and headed toward the river. When he'd gone a short distance beyond the point where the Rio Grande forked, Longarm stopped his search and began retracing his steps to the point where he'd come to the Island.

"Old son," he muttered, "about all a man can hope to do in a place like this is to go prowling on deeper in the brush. Sooner or later, if he keeps zigzagging along, he's going to run into one of the other outlaws that these prints show has got to be holed up around here someplace. Then all that's left to do is get him to show you where the main outlaw hangout is, because that's the most likely place you're apt to find that damn Thad Miller."

Still leading his horse, Longarm set out once more. His progress was slow, for once he'd left the soft yielding clear sandy soil, the dense brush made footprints harder and harder to find. He lost and found the almost invisible trail several times before he'd penetrated the thicket a hundred yards, for on the rising ground the barren sandy soil gave way to dark earth which sustained a thicker fresh green undergrowth. The springy brush masked the surface of the more solid earth away from the shore and did not take footprints as readily.

Though he kept looking for a trail, Longarm did not find one. He kept his eyes fixed on the ground, and while the harder soil of the gently upsloping terrain made his progress easier, the thicker undergrowth kept hampering him. He'd penetrated the thicket for perhaps a quarter of a mile when he reached a small clearing.

Longarm took the opportunity to stop and catch his breath for a moment after his long battle with the under-growth. He looped the horse's reins around the nearest bush, leaned against the hole of a tree, and took out a cigar. He was about to rasp his thumb across the matchhead when a brawny bearded man holding a rifle leveled at Longarm's belt buckle stepped out of the thick underbrush.

"Just stop where you're standing, stranger," the man said. "I ain't seen you on the Island before. Suppose you tell me just who the hell you are and where you come from. And you better be real careful not to make no fast moves. If you're one of us, you're welcome, but if you're a damn lawman I got a bullet here with your name on it, even if I don't know what your name is yet."

Chapter 5

As usual, Longarm thought fast. Keeping his voice at a casually confidential level, he replied, "Now, no offense meant, and I hope you don't object to me saying so, but right now you're acting like a damn trigger-happy lawman yourself. Supposing that I was you, I wouldn't throw down on a man before I'd had a chance to get a half-good look at him."

"I don't take them words kindly, not one bit!" the rifle-man retorted. "If I wasn't a patient man, I'd shoot you without no more palaver on account of what you just said."

"I'll tell you right off that I ain't going to argufy long as I'm looking down the muzzle of that rifle," Longarm replied. He kept his voice at a conversational level as he went on. "Now, if it'll square things up between us, I'll grant you that maybe I was a little bit previous when I said you was trigger-happy. If you had've been, I'd likely be stretched out dead by now. If it's all the same to you, I'll back away and we can start off fresh."

"Meaning what?" the man asked.

"Meaning it sorta looks like I've found the kind of place I've been looking for." Longarm spoke slowly, framing his words carefully. From the first moment that the man holding him at gunpoint had appeared, he'd been sure that his search for the outlaw hideout had ended.

"I take that to mean you're interested in getting to somewheres that's real private?" the rifleman said. "A place where the law ain't apt to come poking into?"

"That's the kind of place I'm looking for, all right," Longarm replied, glad that he could still be truthful without revealing his identity.

"By your looks I'd judge that you're all gringo, so I don't guess it'd be the *rurales* you're running away from. Who's out after you? The sheriff outa El Paso? The Texas Rangers? Or maybe just the railroad dicks?"

"I ain't of a mind to be answering questions, and it don't make no difference who's asking 'em," Longarm said quickly. "The fellow that steered me this way said it was a place where I could go to without anybody asking me what for. Now, it won't do a bit of good for you to start asking who told me that, because I don't aim to pass it on until I know a lot more about who I'm talking to."

"I figure you've already told me what I was trying to find out, so I won't bother to ask you anything else," the man with the rifle said. He was lowering the rifle as he spoke. "And I'll give you good marks for one thing. We don't none of us much like to get asked questions, but you sure know how to answer a man asking 'em without giving much away."

"Now, I take that as being a real polite thing to say,"

Longarm told the outlaw. "But if you're finished asking, I'd like to be sure about one thing."

"And what might that be?"

"I'd feel a lot easier if I was certain this is the place they call the Island," Longarm replied.

"Hell's bells! I thought you knew that! Most everybody that comes here does. Sure, it's the Island. Why?"

"Because it's the place I've been looking for. Like I just said, it won't do you no good to ask me who steered me this way, but I imagine that by now you've got a pretty good idea that I ain't much of a talker."

"I reckon I just have, at that," the man agreed. "But if you've been fretting about where you are, you can set your mind at rest. You've found the Island, all right."

"I was right sure I had, but till you showed up I hadn't run across nobody to ask. I'll feel a mite easier, now that I know I'm in the place that I was told to head for." While he was speaking, Longarm was also cudgeling his brain, trying to dig up a name that would not ring a bell in the outlaw's memory. When none occurred to him he went on. "I was quite some ways off when I remembered that a fellow I knew told me about this place. That's why I'm here now, except that I ain't seen enough of it yet to be sure I'd want to hole up here."

"Sure. I had the same idee, the first time I hit it. But when you see the place we got fixed up, you'll likely feel better about staying. If you don't like our place, there's four more just about like it here on the Island."

"This Island's got to be a pretty good-sized place, then. From what I heard in El Paso, I didn't figure it to be so big."

"It's big enough," the rifleman said. "Two of them other

places I just told you about are bigger'n ours, but they're all pretty much the same except that the others runs more to cross-breeds. At ours, we're Americans—all but one of us, that is."

"Who in the devil is we?"

Looking at Longarm with cold eyes as though to warn him that for a new arrival he was asking too many questions, the rifleman said coldly, "Just some other fellows that needs a quiet place to hole up in for a while."

"That fills my bill, all right. I guess I can count on you to show me where I need to go?" Longarm asked quickly.

"I'll be real glad to do just that. I was just out to stretch my legs a little bit, so I ain't got a horse. Our place ain't but a little piece away from here, not even far enough so's you'll need to mount up. Just lead your nag and follow along."

Nodding in the event that his voice might give some indication of his satisfaction with the offer for which he'd been fishing, Longarm slid his rifle into its saddle scabbard and wrapped the reins of his horse around his left hand. As he led the animal up to the outlaw he said, "Not that it means a whole lot, but if you're getting curious about my name, it's Custis."

"Mine's Beakins, but mostly folks just call me Ab."

Longarm was too wise to push his questioning any further. He acknowledged the outlaw's name with a nod, then flicked his opened hand toward the wall of brush to indicate that he was ready to move. Beakins tucked the butt of his rifle into his elbow, its muzzle slanted toward the ground. Then he turned and started to push his way through the screening vegetation. Longarm picked

58

up the reins of his horse, took the two or three long steps that were needed to close the gap between him and his impromptu guide, and followed the man into the dense greenery of the thicket.

Had he not been accustomed to observing strange trails closely, Longarm might have missed seeing the thread-thin track that Beakins led him over. The trail—if it could be called a trail—was so faintly marked that it could easily have been missed by a foot traveler pushing through the undergrowth for the first time.

Longarm followed his guide through patches of waist-high twisted green weeds and only slightly taller stands of soft green yucca. Now and then they crossed small clearings not much larger than a room, where the ground was hidden by thick curling grass. Two or three times Beakins led them around stands of closely spaced small trees which to Longarm looked like stunted low-growing pines.

They talked little as they moved. The only sounds that disturbed the silence were the occasional whispery swishing of branches disturbed as they pushed through the underbrush and the soft crunching of the horse's hooves. Their progress was slow, and Longarm was beginning to get hungry.

"My belly's starting to think my throat's been cut," he remarked. "If we got much further to go, I'm going to stop and dig some grub outa my saddlebags."

"There won't be any need to stop," Beakins assured him. "The place we're heading for's just a little ways ahead."

"How big of a place is it?" Longarm asked. "And how many's there?" His second question was one he'd been

59

turning over in his mind since they'd started. "The way you talk, I get the idea it's sorta like a town."

"Why, it ain't what you'd call big," the outlaw replied. "Just three cabins and some thatch shelters. They ain't all full, even with the new man that got here yesterday."

Longarm was positive now that his hunch was paying off. He kept his features motionless as he asked, "You sure there'll be room for me?"

"Plenty, even with the new fellow. Counting him, there's only six of us in our stand, but there's two or three more stands along the far side of the Island."

Again Longarm ignored his urge to ask questions about the new arrival, though he was sure it must be Thad Miller. He went on. "Well, I ain't what you'd call choosy. I can spread my bedroll on bare ground and be comfortable enough to sleep sound."

"Oh, you don't need to worry about being crowded. There's plenty of room left under two or three of the shelters," Beakins said. "It don't rain very much here, and it don't hardly ever get real cold, even at night. It ain't but maybe three or four times in dead winter that a man needs to pull a blanket up over him to keep comfortable."

"What about grub and drinking water?"

"Why, there's a little town that ain't too long of a ride down south on the Mexican side of the river. It's called Guadalupe Bravos, and we can get just about all we need there. In winter, when it gets cool enough so fresh meat don't spoil so fast, three or four of us'll borrow a steer from one of the ranches on the Texas side. And we get all the drinking water we need out of a nice clean spring."

"It don't seem to me that a man'd be hard-put to get

60

along, then," Longarm said. "Only six men's staying there?"

"It changes all the time," Beakins replied. "Right now there's only six, but I've seen times when there's been maybe as many as twenty. Thing is, nobody stays long unless they're wanted real bad. Me, now, I been here close to six months."

"Letting the heat die down?"

"What the hell else would keep a man in a place like this? About all you can say is, it beats a jail cell."

"Sure," Longarm agreed. "But I don't aim to stay very long, myself."

"How bad are you wanted?" Beakins asked.

"Why, that'd depend on wherever I might be," Longarm said. Then he added, "But I don't suppose there'd be anybody wanting me where we're heading for, because they wouldn't've had time to get here. I been moving real fast since I left El Paso."

"It's not likely," his outlaw guide agreed. "Not unless you're a damn turncoat or snitch, or a double-crosser that'll go on a job with somebody and try to cheat him out of his fair share of the takings."

Longarm and Beakins had been moving steadily since their start from the edge of the Island. Now Beakins said, "We're just about there."

"It sure took a while," Longarm noted as he swiveled his head from side to side and still saw nothing ahead but the green tangle of semi-tropical brush and trees.

From his years of experience with outlaws, Longarm could understand the real reason why Beakins had been moving so slowly on their way to the hideout. The outlaw had kept them moving at a slower pace than was really required to travel through even the most densely vegatated areas, while he'd been using the time to satisfy himself that he was not leading an informer or a lawman to the place where the other members of his gang were hiding.

"You just ain't looking in the right place," Beakins told him. He pointed. "If you look close up ahead you can see the nearest cabin right between them two trees yonder."

Squinting through the gap in the vegetation which his companion had pointed out, Longarm got his first glimpse of the place he'd set out to find. He saw that Beakins had described it very accurately, and even at first glance he could see that its shelters and cabins were both jerry-built in a manner that could best be described as primitive.

There were a half-dozen tumbledown structures in the outlaw hideaway. Two were cabins, though their small windows had no glass panes and their doors sagged on makeshift leather hinges. Their walls had been cobbled together from boards of a dozen different widths and lengths. The others were merely four tree trunks driven into the ground to serve as posts that supported low shed roofs above a platform of warped planks.

At that, the cabins were only a step or two above the other shelters, which were mere skeletons. The roofs of both cabins and shelters were thatched with layered fronds from the stunted yucca clusters that seemed to thrive in the sandy soil. Stones had been placed in a circle near the center of the clearing. A few iron pots and a skillet resting on them told Longarm that the ring was used as a cooking fire. At the edge of the cleared area a pole corral confined two horses. As far as he could see, there was no one moving in the vicinity.

"Well?" Beakins asked. "Think the place'll be good enough to suit you?"

"From here, it looks fine, and I ain't much of a one to be choosy," Longarm answered. "But there don't seem to be nobody around. If I ain't forgot, you said a while ago that there's six of you."

"I guess I didn't think to mention it," the outlaw replied. "The other fellows have gone down to Guadalupe Bravos. That's the little Mexican town I told you about that's on the river a ways south of here."

"They ain't going to do nothing there that'd stir up the *rurales,* are they? Like maybe a bank job?"

"Hell, no!" Beakins replied quickly. "We're smart enough not to piss in our own bed. Like when we go to El Paso, there ain't but two or three of us goes at one time. You know yourself, Custis, when a bunch of men rides into a little place like that there's folks that'll be noticing 'em right off."

"That makes good sense," Longarm agreed.

"Now, in Guadalupe Bravos it's different," the outlaw said. "The only law there's one *rurale* who's half-drunk or asleep most of the time when he ain't out riding patrol. So that's where we go when the grub box is damn near empty and we run plumb outa liquor. But besides that, there was some of the boys that was getting awful horny. They got to talking about the girls in the little whorehouse down there, and the first thing you know they was saddling up."

"How come you didn't go along with 'em?"

"Because I cut low card when we was drawing to see

who'd stay behind and mind this place here, damn it!"

"Well, now," Longarm said. "That eases my mind a lot. I been on the prod a mite too long, and I'd a sight rather stop someplace where it's safe to stay and rest a while."

"Well, our place is going to be real quiet till the others get back. You won't have nothing to do but rest."

"I reckon you know just the same as I do that when a man's on the run he'll hole up just about anyplace where he can rest for a while," Longarm said. "That is, anyplace where he won't be having to look over his shoulder all the time so's he can make sure there ain't nobody following him."

"Sure," the outlaw agreed. "It's likely you've seen just the same as I have what happens to us when we get too set in our ways. Some damn lawman tumbles to where we are, or a snitching turncoat tells him where he can figure to run us down, and that's the end of us."

"You don't suppose there'll be a lawman lucky enough to find this place, do you?" Longarm hoped that he was showing a proper degree of alarm, a state of mind that expressed a mild anxiety rather than fear of an encounter.

"Hell, the law knows we're here," Beakins snorted.

"That don't sound too good to me," Longarm said with a frown.

"I'm talking now about the American law in El Paso and the *rurales* in Juarez and Chihuahua," Beakins replied. "But both of 'em leaves us pretty much alone. There ain't many lawmen close by that likes to take all the trouble it is to get here. That's what's holding 'em back."

64

"Maybe I'll just stay here long enough to catch my breath," Longarm said as he turned away from his inspection of the outlaw's hideout. "I been on the prod for quite a spell, long enough so's I figure I got a little rest coming."

"If it's rest you're after, you'll have plenty of time for it," Beakins assured him. "Till the others get back, of course."

"You got a job figured out that you're going to pull sometime soon?"

"Not yet. But pretty quick we got to figure out what our next one's going to be, on account of we're running sorta short of cash."

"That ought not to be too hard to cure," Longarm suggested, playing his assumed role of an outlaw on the run. "It ain't all that far to El Paso, and—"

"We don't mess with El Paso," Beakins broke in. "It's too damn close to the Island here."

"As far as I know, it's the only place nearby that's got banks and places like 'em that's worth wasting time on."

"Oh, you're right about that," Beakins agreed. "But there's way too many lawmen there too."

"Hell, you're going to find them bastards everyplace!" Longarm said, keeping up his pose as an outlaw, and hoping privately that his words would never be repeated where any of his fellow lawmen might hear them.

"Not as many as El Paso's got for a place its size," Beakins replied. "They got a town marshal and a sheriff and even a federal marshal's office now. All of them are real hardcased gunfighters too."

"I still say it's the only place where there'd be enough

65

of a haul to make a job worth bothering with," Longarm insisted.

"And I don't say you ain't right," Beakins agreed. "We've jawed a lot about El Paso and a good-sized bunch of other places where we might score a hit, but we ain't made up our minds yet."

"Well, from what little you've told me, you got enough men here for a big job," Longarm said. "And somebody's bound to come up with a scheme."

"Oh, sure," Beakins agreed. "Should push come to shove, all of us has got stashes with plenty of money piled away, but none of 'em's close enough for us to get at easy."

They'd reached the outlaw camp by this time. Longarm saw nothing that he hadn't noted when examining the place before, though the jerry-built nature of the two cabins was much more obvious than it had been when he'd been looking from a distance.

"I feel like I'm about ready to take a little rest," he told Beakins. "Just you show me where to bunk down, then I'll spread out my bedroll and catch forty winks."

"There was a spare cot in one of them shacks till that new fellow come in," Beakins replied. Frowning thoughtfully, he went on. "But about the best you can do now is bunk in one of the open-sided ones. There's room in both of them, so it don't make much difference which one you pick out. If you don't feel like bedding down right away, there's still some stew left in the cooking pot, if you'd like to eat before you rest."

"I reckon I'm tireder than I am hungry," Longarm said. He indicated the open-sided shelter that was nearest the edge of the clearing. "So since it don't make no never

66

mind, suppose we put off palavering till after a while and I'll spread my bedroll in that place over yonder and get in a little shut-eye."

"You do whatever suits you. But you keep thinking over that job I mentioned, and when the rest of the boys get back we'll do some more talking about it."

Chapter 6

Longarm put his horse in the pole corral after Beakins had left to go to his own quarters. Always mindful of the need for a man in his position to be familiar with his surroundings—especially in such dangerous situations as the one in which he now found himself—he took time to inspect the area around the enclosure.

He discovered quickly that there were two paths leading from it into the thick vegetation. They showed only lightly in the dense growth of tall weeds and grasses, but both led into the tangled green thickness of the brush. Realizing that with night so near he could not spare the time to follow either of the little trails and find out where they led, Longarm noted the dim pathways in his mind for a detailed exploration as soon as possible. He returned to the corral, and was starting toward the shelter where his bedroll waited when he came across a stretch of ground where some sort of coarse grass grew thick and waist-high.

Along the margin of the patch, the withered stubs of plucked grass-shoots provided a clue that the outlaws must have been feeding the grass to their horses. Longarm quickly pulled enough grass to let his own mount feed without foundering, and dropped it in the corral where he'd left his horse. Then, shouldering his saddlebags and bedroll, he stepped across the clearing to the sheltered platform.

"Well, old son," he muttered to himself when a quick glance told him that Beakins had disappeared into one of the cabins, "even if you've found the place you set out to look for, you ain't seen hide nor hair of that damned Thad Miller yet. Which means he's bound to've got here in time to ride down to that place Beakins was talking about. But it wasn't the time to get real nosey when Beakins said what he did."

After a moment of silent work while he was loosening the leather thongs that were tied around his bedroll, and spreading it on the floor of the shelter, Longarm began one of his muttered colloquies with himself.

"You know, old son," he began, "when push comes to shove, it might just be a good thing you ain't see hide nor hair of that Miller fellow yet. You've beat the odds so far, and luck's got a real mean habit of turning when a man ain't looking for it to. Now, there's a few things you better keep in mind. One of 'em is that the only turn this case can take now has got to be for the better. And the other one is that you'll feel better after you've had a little shut-eye."

Spreading his blankets on a strip of unoccupied space at the edge of the platform, Longarm levered off his boots, stretched out luxuriously on the bedroll, and within a few moments was asleep.

•   •   •

It seemed to Longarm that he'd barely closed his eyes when a noise broke the dusk's stillness. Though it was only a faint whisperlike sound, it jarred him into full and instant wakefulness. Sitting up, he glanced around quickly. The sun's rays glowed now on only the tops of the tallest trees, but there was enough light trickling into the clearing to allow him to see his surroundings quite plainly.

As Longarm rose he'd reached for the Colt that had been resting beside the folded saddle pad he'd been using for a pillow. The revolver was in his hand and his eyes were searching the deepening shadows that had veiled the surrounding undergrowth only a few seconds after the sound of careful footfalls and the whispers of rustling bushes had reached his ears.

"Not to eshoot! I don' come to hurt nobody, an' not to esteal too!"

To Longarm's surprise, the heavily accented voice coming from the dense brush was that of a woman. He did not lower the muzzle of his revolver. Instead, he swiveled in a half turn, peering in the direction from which the voice had sounded.

In the growing duskiness of failing half-light that was settling in on the clearing, he could barely make out the form of the woman who'd spoken. Although she was only a dozen or so paces from the edge of the platform where he'd been sleeping, the deep shadows cast by the wall of brush behind her and the tree tops that rose above the undergrowth hid the details of her face and figure.

But in spite of the darkness and distance between them, Longarm could see her dimly. He could tell that she was of medium height, had dark hair that fell behind her,

71

and wore a *china poblano* costume, a thin loosely fitting white blouse and a dark-colored very full knee-length skirt. She had on huaraches, but no stockings.

"I ain't the kinda man that'd shoot a woman," Longarm told her. "Not even when they come sneakin' up on a man while he's asleep. But before you get any closer, maybe you better tell me who you are and what you come here for."

"My name ees Rosalita," she replied without hesitation. "But I do not see you here on the Island until now."

"Likely that's because I ain't been here before," he replied. "I just rode in a little while ago. And I sure wasn't looking for nobody to come visiting."

"Ees here I am come wheen I am *abatido,* like now."

Longarm's knowledge and use of Spanish was limited, but the woman had used one of the words that happened to be in his vocabulary. He frowned as he asked, "You're saying you just come here on account of you're lonesome?"

"*De seguro,*" she replied. "From where I am estay all of the meen have gone, now are only there *las mujeres.*"

"So you live here on the Island?"

"*Si, al otro lado—*" She stopped short and repeated in English, "By the other side from the reever."

Longarm nodded. "You mean you live over there in a place like this one here?"

"*Seguro,*" she repeated. "Ees more as one *campamento* like thees on *la isla, y soy islana.* Bot I am come to here other times."

"Then I reckon that sorta makes us neighbors, Rosalita." Longarm smiled. Relaxed now, he took out a cigar and flicked a match into flame to light it.

During their brief talk, Rosalita had taken two or three short careful steps forward. She stood now in front of the edge of the darkening shadows cast by the vegetation, and in the better light Longarm could see her more clearly. She could have been any age from her late teens to her early twenties. Her eyes seemed overlarge, for in the fading light their irises had dilated until their whites became only narrow glints between them and her long lashes.

Longarm puffed out a small cloud of smoke and took his cigar from his mouth. Then he said, "Well, if you just come to visit, I sure don't mind a bit. Suppose you come over here and set down by me, if you've a mind to. It'll beat talking loud, like we got to now."

Without hesitation or comment, Rosalita stepped up to the little shelter. When only a yard or two separated her from Longarm she whirled around, and the movement sent her skirt flaring upward. It stood out far enough from her legs to reveal that they were bare and plump, and the clinging of her low-cut blouse as she turned hinted at generous breasts. She settled on the platform's edge. Longarm stood looking at her for a moment. Then he sat down beside her, not too closely, but with a span of a foot or more between them.

"From what you was telling me a minute ago, I gather you come over here every now and then," he said. "Not looking for nothing or nobody special?"

"Wheen the men from where I estay all ride away, I am make tired by leesten to the talk-talk-talk of women," she replied.

"So what you really come over here for is to find a man you can visit with?"

For a moment Rosalita was silent while she examined Longarm with unconcealed curiosity. He did not speak or move during the time when her eyes were flicking over him, and Longarm was as silent as she was.

"My name I am to tell you wheen you ask me," she reminded him without answering his question. "You do not tell me yours, bot first you tell me you eshoot me, theen you are start to ask me question wheen I do not even know who I am e-talk weeth. I think I do not weesh to speak more weeth you."

"Hold on, now, Rosalita!" Longarm exclaimed. "I got to admit you're right, it wasn't real polite of me not to tell you my name when we begun talking. But—" He stopped short and shook his head, then went on. "And here I am, spouting off with my mouth again when I oughta be asking you to excuse me when I was sorta rude. Now, I beg your pardon for that. Call me Custis, and excuse me for not being polite."

Rosalita stood in thoughtful silence for a moment or two; then she smiled to show dazzling white teeth and nodded. "I weel take your apology, Custis," she said as she moved closer to him. "And now I weel answer the questions you are ask me."

"Now, there ain't no reason why you got to tell me one single thing," Longarm told her quickly. "It ain't rightly none of my affair, and was you to ask me why I was here, I reckon I'd feel just about the same as you did when I was poking into your private business."

"Theen I weel guess why you are here," she said. "Ees eet not that you are *amigo* weeth the men who are estay here?"

"Well, I wouldn't put it perzactly that way," Longarm

replied. "Seeing as how I only met up with one of 'em so far."

"Thees one ees Beekings?"

"Sure. If you get here once in a while, I reckon you know he's the only one of 'em that's here right now."

"I am hear that some are go to Guadalupe Bravos. I do not know how many."

"Now, how'd you happen to hear that?"

"Een place like thees, nobody have secret. We see, we talk, we leesten. Pretty queek, everybody ees know."

"I reckon you're right about that, Rosalita," Longarm agreed. "But how'd you happen to come over here when you knew all them fellows was gone?"

"Ees always one who estay here. They don't got things to do, like wheen all men are here. Theen one who estay ees glad to see me if I come here."

"What you're saying is that you come to hustle up some business, then?"

She shook her head. "No. I am not for men to buy, like they do *las putas*. Wheen I make love weeth man, ees because I like to. Ees for good time, not money."

"Well, now," Longarm said. "If that's what you're after, seeing as we ain't run into each other before now, I reckon it's Beakins you're looking for. Like I said, him and me's the only ones here."

"Theen I weel estay weeth you," Rosalita announced. "Heem I do not like. I know he ees so old he ees *ningun bueno* when he try to make love."

"For all you know, maybe I ain't much *bueno* neither."

"Eef for myself I must find out, theen thees es what I weel do," she told Longarm.

75

Rosalita was smiling as she spoke. Her hand moved to his crotch and she began exploring the vee of his thighs. Longarm made no effort to stop his response. When she felt him beginning to swell, Rosalita abandoned the dancing movements of her fingers and gave closer attention to the burgeoning cylinder that was now beginning to show as it swelled in response to her continuing caresses.

Longarm waited only a moment before beginning his own explorations. Tossing his cigar butt aside, he slid his hands up the thin loose fabric of her blouse and cradled her generous breasts, rubbing and caressing them until he felt their tips bud and grow firm. Rosalita threw back her head and offered him her lips. Longarm accepted the unspoken invitation, and when her jutting tongue parted his lips, he met it with his. Their caresses grew prolonged, and when they broke apart both Longarm and Rosalita sat motionless and gasping for a few moments.

She was the first to move. Standing up, she shrugged out of her loose blouse. It fell and dangled from the waist of her skirt. Longarm could see now that her breasts were very full and that her dark rosettes were pebbled around puckered protruding tips.

When she settled beside him again, Rosalita's hand moved to Longarm's crotch. He did not try to evade her touch as she caressed his beginning erection, and after a moment she unbuckled his belt and loosed the buttons of his trousers to push them down. Now she groped for his erection and freed it, and started stroking it softly. Longarm bent his head to kiss her again, and this time her tongue darted into his mouth.

He opened his lips too and met it with his. Rosalita's fingers were busy at his crotch, and after a moment she gripped it firmly as she began to writhe gently. She turned her head slightly to break their kiss, and when their lips parted said, "Your bedroll ees very close. Eet ees better place for us than the ground."

Lifting Rosalita in his muscular arms, Longarm took the few short steps across the platform to his bedroll. He lowered her to her feet. Rosalita locked one arm around Longarm's shoulders, and before he could begin to lower her to the heap of touseled blankets, she raised herself by levering with her arm and reached down to place him as she wrapped her legs around his hips.

Longarm dropped to his knees when she leaned back, and when she reached the waiting blankets he fell forward and arched his back to drive fully into her. Rosalita cried out with a throbbing ululation as Longarm completed his lunge, but one such deep sudden thrust was not enough to please her. Before he could place his knees to drive again, she released the pressure of her legs and spread them wide.

She gasped, "Fast and deep and do not e-stop, even eef I beg you to!"

Longarm was more than ready to respond to Rosalita's urging. He plunged again and again while she brought up her hips to meet his thrusts and inarticulate bubbling sighs of pleasure broke from her throat. Her head arched back, her eyes were squeezed shut, and her generous red lips twisted as she matched Longarm's drives, raising her hips to meet his lusty thrusting.

Suddenly her body grew rigid and her hips began to jerk out of rhythm with Longarm's lunges. Her cries of delight had been bubbling soft; now they grew in a mounting crescendo of delight. Her body quivered and the lifting motion of her hips began jerking out of rhythm with Longarm's thrusts.

Then Rosalita screamed, and as her voice rose she released one arm to cover her mouth with her hand. As Longarm maintained his steady pounding, her body jerked and she writhed beneath him as their rhythm broke and she squirmed as though trying to escape him, but all the while her legs were locking him to her more desperately.

Even when Rosalita relaxed and her body grew limp as her cries died away, Longarm continued his steady full-length rhythmic thrusts, though at a more leisurely pace. Soon Rosalita's muscles began functioning again. She rose to a climax faster than she had before, and this time when her frantic spasms mounted to a climax, Longarm let his own control go and joined with her in a frantic consummation.

They separated then and lay quietly apart, with small tremors twitching them occasionally until their breathing returned to its normal regular pace. Rosalita was the first to speak.

"You weel be on the Island for a while?" she asked.

"That's something I can't tell you for a while yet," he replied. "After the other fellows get back, I oughta know."

"Theen I weel come veesit you," she promised. "But now let us sleep and perhaps wheen we wake again—"

"No perhaps about it," Longarm said. "Count on it as a promise. If you wake up before I do, just give me a little poke and I'll be ready to start over again."

•   •   •

"I sure would like to know what's keeping them boys in that little jerkwater town such a long time." Ab Beakins frowned as he and Longarm sat sipping coffee after a make-do breakfast of bacon scraps fried with the remainder of yesterday's boiled rice. "They got to know I'd be scraping bottom on my grub box by this time, long as they been gone."

"Like I told you when you come looking to see if I wanted to eat breakfast with you, I got enough grub in my saddlebags to feed us maybe two or three days, if we're careful," Longarm said.

"Oh, I didn't forget," Beakins replied. "And if they don't get back here today, we might just need to break into what you got. But mainly what I'm fretting over is why they're staying. If they started some kinda ruckus down there in Guadalupe Bravos, the *rurales* might've tossed 'em in jail."

"Do the *rurales* give you much trouble here?"

"They sure ain't been around much lately. From what I hear, the *rurales* is keeping pretty busy riding patrol on that new railroad line that the Mescins is pushing up from Chihuahua City to El Paso."

"All the same, it sounds to me like this ain't the safest place to hole up in."

"Hell, it always has been. Nobody knows for sure whether it's in *rurales* or Ranger territory, so both of 'em sorta fights shy of it."

"Just the same, I'll see how thing turn out for a few days," Longarm said. "I don't know much about this place, except I've heard it's a good place to hole up."

"I been here a pritty good spell," Beakins said. "Maybe too long of a while. My name's on too many wanted posters. Some's even got my picture on 'em. I still got to hide out a spell longer before they fade and gets throwed away. I don't figure to pull out till I get chased out or starved out."

Beakins stood up and stretched. "I reckon I'll amble over to my cabin and stretch out. That is, if you're going to be around to sorta keep an eye on things."

"Go right ahead. I had all the shut eye I needed last night, so I'll just laze around. But that won't stop me from keeping my eyes peeled. If I run across anything—"

Longarm broke off as a frown suddenly formed on Beakins's face and the old outlaw swiveled around to peer through the growth behind them. Longarm got to his feet and stepped to the old outlaw's side. Beakins had raised his hand to rest it on the butt of his holstered revolver.

"You hear something I didn't?" Longarm asked.

"I ain't sure yet, but—" Beakins was still resting his hand on his pistol butt, his head thrust forward. "When you're hiding out in a place like this, you never know who might be prowling around. It might be all I heard was a deer or something like that."

"A deer won't generally make no noise unless it's got spooked. And I got pretty good ears, but I didn't hear a thing."

"Maybe I didn't either," Beakins replied. "But I ain't one to make that kind of—"

He broke off as a rustle of leaves and branches sounded from the dense thicket between them and the river. Then a man's voice came from the green wall of entangled underbrush.

"Stir up the fire, Ab! It's us come back and we got a real fine load of grub!"

80

Chapter 7

"It's a good thing your friends let us know when they did that it was them making all that noise," Longarm remarked, dropping his hand from the butt of his Colt. "I was just about ready to let a few slugs loose."

"And I was just getting ready to knock your gun away," Beakins said. "I've heard them brushes scraping enough times so it don't spook me now that I'm used to it."

"Well, now, I wasn't exactly spooked," Longarm noted. "But you know just like I do that when a man's on the prod it don't take a hell of a lot to get him a mite edgy."

"Oh, I'll grant you that a bunch of fellows leading their horses through the brush makes a real foofaraw. A'course, I had it all figured out that it couldn't be nobody but them even before Smokey yelled at us."

While they talked the noise in the bushes had come closer. Before Longarm could reply, the first of the outlaws entered the clearing.

Beakins went on. "Sure enough, that's old Smokey now. He's in a hurry most all the time."

Longarm watched the remaining men as one by one they broke through the dense vegetation and started leading their horses across the cleared ground. He hid the feeling of relief that swept over him when he did not recognize any of the three who had followed the outlaw Beakins had hailed as Smokey. Then a frown began to form on his face when no fifth man emerged from the straggling wall of brush and the sounds of disturbed branches died away.

As the four new arrivals led their horses toward him and Beakins, Longarm did not allow his face to reflect the disappointed frustration he was feeling at that moment. He accepted the unpleasant fact that Thad Miller was not with the gang.

Beakins was already advancing to greet his companions. Longarm saw the outlaw point toward him, and judged the newcomers were being told who he was and what he was doing on the Island. His quick estimate of the situation proved to be accurate when the group stopped a few paces in front of him and Beakins turned to the others.

"This is Custis, the fellow I been telling you about," he announced. "He rode in while you was gone." He turned to face Longarm and went on, indicating the newcomers as he called their names. "Custis, this big geezer here's Dunlap. That one's Mahan, and I told you a minute ago who Smokey is. And this other one's Carlos."

Longarm had nodded as each of the men was introduced. He did not allow his feeling of disappointment to show on his face, and did not extend his hand to be shaken, nor did he make the mistake of asking about the missing Thad Miller. He studied the four new arrivals with quick flicks of his ice-blue eyes while Beakins was ticking off their names.

Dunlap was an oversized man, and though he had a potbelly that hung over his belt and came close to hiding its elaborate silver buckle, he was not a fat man in the true sense of the word. Like all the others except Smokey, he was freshly shaved. The bulges of his biceps and the heavy broad ridges of thigh muscles outlined by the tight legs of his denim jeans told their own story of strength.

Mahan stood next to Dunlap, dwarfed by the big man's size. Although he looked small in comparison, and actually stood a half-head shorter than the men around him, Mahan's face bore a grim look even when he smiled. His cheeks were ridged with the weals of long-healed scars. One of the long bulges slanted down a cheek from the outside corner of his eyes almost to the point of his jutting jaw. On the other cheek, a similar scar ran in a half circle from the center of his ear to the midpoint of his jaw. Where the scar began the lobe of his ear was missing.

Smokey appeared to be the oldest of the four outlaws. He had a brushy beard and a straggly gray mustache, long untrimmed, that overlapped his upper lip and hid its contours. A jutting pointed jaw turned his face into an elongated oval. His eyebrows were finger-thick wads of gray above a pair of the coldest blue eyes that Longarm had ever encountered.

Carlos was clearly the youngest of the quartet. His weather-tanned cheeks showed fewer creases and his skin was a half-shade darker than that of his companions. His face bore only one scar, a small and narrow but prominent weal that angled across one of his high cheekbones. His jaws were stubbled with a two-day growth of midnight-black whiskers and his thick eyebrows above dark eyes were as black as the carefully trimmed mustache that swept across his upper lip. Carlos's nose was in the best Hispanic tradition, a straight narrow line from his brow to the bulge of his heavy mustache.

There was little difference in the clothing worn by the quartet. All four of the outlaws had on much-used and tightly fitting Levi's blue denim saddle jeans, the trouser legs tucked into the tops of their boots.

Their shirts did not match as well as their breeches did. Dunlap was the only one who whose shirt echoed the blue denim of his jeans. Mahan had on a black shirt, spotted here and there with a patch of white where sweat had dried. Smokey's shirt had once been a rainbow of bright red, blue, green, and yellow checks, but now it was faded so badly that the colors no longer warred with one another and almost seemed compatible. Carlos's shirt was a relatively new one of billowing brown satin that still had some of its pristine sheen.

All four of the men had gunbelts on, the revolvers dangling low on their thighs in scarred and scuffed leather holsters, the barrel-ends of the holsters secured by leather thongs above the knee. The butts of all four revolvers bore the shine of long and regular use.

Longarm's examination of the outlaw quartet was quick but not cursory. Beakins was just beginning to explain what had happened while the others had been away. While he talked, Longarm was examining the new arrivals with quick unobtrusive flicks of his ice-blue eyes.

"Custis blew in here looking for a hidey-hole the other day," Beakins was saying now. Then a frown rippled his brow and he asked, "What in hell happened to that Miller fellow that went with you? You-all didn't stomp up a ruckus while you was down at Guadalupe Bravos and get in trouble with the *alcalde*, did you?"

"Now, you know we been dodging lawmen long enough so's we wouldn't do some damn-fool thing that'd make 'em notice us, Ab," Mahan replied.

Dunlap chimed in quickly to say, "All we done besides buying grub was have a few drinks and get our ashes hauled in the whorehouse a time or two. But about the time we was getting ready to start back, that Miller fellow got hisself a bad case of itchy feet. He told us he wasn't of a mind to spend no more time on the Island."

"You mean you left Miller there in Guadalupe Bravos?" Beakins asked. The frown that had almost disappeared from his face suddenly returned. "If he's wanted bad as he made hisself out to be, the *rurales* might grab him, and with all the ways they've got of making a man talk—"

"Now, don't go getting your bowels in an uproar," Smokey said, breaking in. "We told him where he'd have to watch out for off-trails and which side of all the forks he'd be having to take to Chihuahua City. If he does just like we said he'd have to, he'll make it all the way there."

"Hell, we even done more'n what Smokey let on," Mahan volunteered. "We rode with Miller for a little ways out of town to be sure he got started on the right road to Chihuahua City."

Seeing the look of incredulity that was forming on Beakins's face, Smokey said, "We done our best trying to tell him he was making a damn fool move, but he wasn't of a mind to listen to us."

"That's right," Dunlap agreed. "And I'd guess he's a good part of the way there by now if he didn't make some fool mistake like blowing his horse and likely foundering it if he tries to go too fast over them steep ridges between here and there."

"That road don't go through much besides desert country, as I recall it," Beakins said slowly. "There ain't none too many water holes along it, and him being by hisself—"

"Thees we try to e-tell heem," Carlos interrupted. "He ees not listen, the more *tonto* he got to be."

"It ain't nothing off our plate anyways," Dunlap said. "We wasn't counting on him being along when we started getting the job pulled together."

"Dunlap's right," Smokey agreed. "We'll do just as good without him as we would've if he went with us."

Longarm had masked his growing interest in the outlaws' conversation by taking out one of his long thin cigars and lighting it, but he had been listening carefully to what they'd said. Now he decided it was time for him to step into a firmer position with the gang in order to learn more about Thad Miller's plans than would be possible in his present pose as an outsider.

"I ain't trying to be pushy," he said after blowing out a shimmering cloud of cigar smoke. "But if you're needing another man to fill out on this job you been scheming up—"

Beakins broke in. "I was just about to say something like that myself." Turning to face his fellow outlaws, he went on. "From what little I've seen of Custis since he's

86

been here, I figure we could count on him hauling his own weight and maybe a little bit more if he was in a mind to join in with us."

"We don't need to be in a hurry to decide nothing right now," Mahan told his companions. "Me, I'm ready to sack out for a good long spell, now we're back here where a man don't have to sleep with one eye open all the time. I sure ain't aiming to stand around here while we keep on palavering about what we might do or might not do."

"That's about how I feel too," Smokey said, seconding the other outlaw's remark. "I'm aiming to get in some of the shut-eye we missed while we was seeing the elephant and listening to the owl down there at Guadalupe Bravos. I'm heading for my bedroll."

"What Mahan's said hits the mark with me," Dunlap agreed. "It ain't like we got to make up our minds in none too big of a hurry, and I'd as lief be in my bedroll as not right now."

"I'd say that goes for all of us, except maybe Ab," Mahan said. "All I got pushing at me is my belly griping on account of it being empty. The only thing we et on the way back here was some tortillas and a bite or two of jerky. Right now, what's on my mind is a mouthful or two of something that'll stop my belly-gripes. Then I aim to sleep till about this time tomorrow."

"Well, you know what it'll take to stop them gripes," Beakins told him. "It's victuals in your belly instead of air. And you fellows better have what we need in your saddlebags, because we're sure scraping bottom for grub."

"We are bring back so much as we can put in *las*

alforjas," Carlos assured him. "And I am eesy like the others. Now, we e-sleep. *Mas tarde,* we talk."

"Well, I sure as hell ain't going to hit the sack till I've got something to eat," Mahan insisted. "And we still got our horses to unsaddle and our bedrolls to spread." Turning to Beakins, he said, "Ab, why don't you and Custis see what you can find in them saddlebags while we get settled down. Then we'll all rest after we've et."

"That'd be the sensible thing to do," Beakins agreed. "Tell you what, me and Custis here don't need no more shut-eye right now. We had brains enough to go to bed when it was dark. If he's agreeable, me and him can take care of emptying the grub you brought back out of your saddlebags while you're taking care of your little chores and getting shed of your trail dust."

"You don't hear me saying that I ain't ready to help," Longarm put in quickly.

"There ain't nothing but the grub in my saddlebags," Mahan said. "You can take it out of 'em whenever you're ready. Now that our ride's over, I'm going to have a good spell of not doing nothing."

"Me too," Dunlap agreed. "And while you're at it, I'd be obliged if you'll take the grub outa my saddlebags too. I never was much of a hand at cooking. If I had my druthers all the time, I wouldn't do doing anything but eat what somebody else has cooked."

"Why, any man'd be a plain damn fool to turn down a deal like that," Smokey said. "I'll go right along with everybody else."

"*Es verdad,*" Carlos agreed. "But I must do one small theeng before I can e-rest. My horse ees got stone een between eets shoe and hoof, so I got to take out or eet goes lame. So queek as I do thees, then I e-rest too."

"Looks like I talked us into a job, Custis," Beakins said, turning to Longarm as the others scattered out, heading away to take care of their mounts. "I wasn't aiming to tangle you up in it when I begun talking, it all just sorta busted out."

"Why, that don't faze me one little bit," Longarm assured the outlaw. "Me and Dunlap's the same. I ain't such a much when it comes to cooking. But I guess I'm purty near as hungry as everybody else is, so whenever you're ready to start getting the grub ready, all you got to do is yell at me if you need somebody to lend you a hand."

"Tell you what," Beakins said. "If you'll just do a little bit of a chore to help me, I'll handle the cooking part by myself."

"My word's good," Longarm replied. "You tell me what you'd like for me to do."

"These saddlebags look like the belly of a she-wolf that's getting ready to drop her cubs," Beakins said. "I'd be obliged if you'll give me a hand lugging 'em over to where the cooking-fire is."

"Why, that ain't such a much. You pick up two, and I'll lug the other two."

"And there's a mite more I'll ask you to help me with when we've got these saddlebags moved," the outlaw continued as they started away, each man carrying a pair of saddlebags in each hand.

"Just sing out," Longarm invited.

"Well, there never is a time when a man that's cooking don't need water. You know by now where the spring is, so if you'll go—"

"Sure. How much water you figure to need?"

"Oh, a couple of bucketsful is all. And them two little chores is about all I can think of right now," Beakins added. "Except we'll have these saddlebags to unload."

"Then we might as well do that first," Longarm suggested. "Once you know what's in 'em, it'll be easier for you to figure out what you wanta fix."

"So I will. Let's get at it, then. I'll empty out Mahan's and the one I lent to him so's they'd have room to carry a bigger load while you tend to Smokey's and Carlos's."

Hunkering down, they began unloading the saddlebags. The first bundle that Longarm took out of the bag he'd chosen was swathed in tattered threadbare cloth over a thick layer of coarse straw. While he was pulling the straw aside to lessen the bulk of the package, Beakins glanced over. He was just in time to see Longarm pull the straw aside and reveal the rounded ends of several brown eggshells.

"Now, ain't that a sight for sore eyes!" Beakins exclaimed. "Real hen's eggs! Why, I ain't had a fried egg since we holed up here! You just let me have them hen fruits, Custis. I know right this minute what we're going to eat soon as I can get some grease bubbling in the skillet!"

Handing Beakins the bulky package, Longarm pulled out the next bundle. It was grease-stained and slippery, and even before he'd begun to unwrap the cloth around it he knew by the smell what he was handling.

"Here's the bacon to go with the eggs," he told Beakins. "Hadn't you best frizzle up a slice or two of it and get a mite of grease to cook them eggs in?"

"Sure," Beakins agreed. He held up the package he'd been opening before Longarm displayed the eggs. "And look at this, Custis! Bread, real bread, not tortillas or hotcakes, a whole damn big loaf of it! Why, just looking at all this kinda grub's got my juices running!"

"I got to admit it, I'd enjoy a meal like that myself," Longarm agreed.

"Well, it'll cook up quick, and the others'll all sleep better if they got their bellies full. Tell you what, Custis, on your way to the spring, you tell the fellows what I'm going to cook up, and tell 'em to hop on over here to eat before they start catching up on their shut-eye."

"Glad to," Longarm agreed. "And I'll fetch the water back."

Longarm started taking long strides toward the spring, swinging the water bucket as he walked. He'd covered almost half the distance when he encountered Mahan and Dunlap, angling off toward their cabin. After hearing the words "eggs" and "bacon" they changed direction and started for the cooking fire. A few moments later he ran into Smokey, strolling slowly away from the corral.

"Ab said to tell you he's cooking eggs and bacon," Longarm said. "And I don't reckon you'd wanta miss out on 'em."

"Not so's you'd notice," Smokey replied. "When all the hogs are at the trough, I aim to be right with 'em."

"You go on, then," Longarm told him. "I still got to find Carlos, but I ain't run into him yet. You don't know if he's asleep or not, I guess?"

"You'll find him at the corral," Smokey said. "He's still fussing around with that nag of his, trying to get its hoof fixed up."

"Good. I'll go ahead get him and by the time we get back the grub oughta be ready."

Covering the remaining distance to the corral, Longarm found Carlos standing beside his horse, rubbing his hands along the sides of his trousers.

"You finished working on your critter?" Longarm asked.

"*Sí,* the rock een hees hoof I have just get out," Carlos replied. "And like the *lobo* I am hongry."

"Then you better mosey on back to the cookfire with me," Longarm said. "Because I that's where I just sent the other fellows. They didn't waste no time when I told 'em Ab's cooking eggs and bacon for breakfast."

"They are all at the fire, then?" Carlos asked, his eyes fixed on Longarm's face.

"Sure. Everybody's there but you and me."

"This ees good," Carlos replied. "Eet geeves me chance to do what I am waiting for."

"What might that be?" Longarm frowned.

"*Un momento,*" Carlos replied. He was unbuckling his belt as he spoke.

A frown formed on Longarm's face as Carlos began pulling his wide deeply tooled belt out of its supporting straps.

"You mind telling me—" Longarm began.

"*Momento, amigo,*" Carlos said. "You weel esee why I do thees thing."

By this time, Longarm's frown was fully formed. He said, "Now, hold on, Carlos! I ain't one bit—"

He stopped short and his eyes widened as Carlos finished removing the belt and turned its inner side to face Longarm. Pinned to the belt's inner surface there was a golden badge. Longarm needed no second look. He had seen identical badges before. It was the one worn by high-ranking officers of Mexico's feared *rurales*.

Chapter 8

For a few seconds Longarm stood with his mouth half-open, staring at the gleaming golden badge.

Carlos said quickly, "Do not be of concern, Marshal Long. I have wanted thees badge to eshow you wheen I see you the first time, but until now there ees no time or place I can do eet without others seeing eet as well."

Longarm's jaw dropped still lower, then he recovered from his second surprise in as many minutes and said, "You're telling me you've knowed all the time who I am?"

"*Seguro que si,*" Carlos said. "But I theenk eet ees not so easy for you to remember me. Maybe so eef I remind you of a jail in our country some years past, and of a *rurale capitan* name Sanchez. Heem you weel remember, and that you do not get along so good weeth heem—"

"Hell's bells!" Longarm broke in. "That sure was a real long time back, but I ain't forgot it yet! You mean you was in the *rurales* then?"

"Theen, I am new recruit," Carlos replied. "And I do not like Sanchez more as you do. He ees bring no honor to our *rurale* force. But he ees dead now, keel by one of hees own men. And I, myself, am now *capitan*."

Longarm took another good look at Carlos; then he nodded and asked, "There can't be but one reason why you're working undercover on the Island, then. You got to be after one of the fellows in this gang that's hiding out here."

"You are make the good guess," Carlos said. "But eet ees all of theem. I am here weeth these *bandidos* by the especial order from the *comandante en jefe* of my force to estop the raids they make into my country."

"So you got to go along into Mexico," Longarm noted. "On account of it's the only way you can get the evidence you need?"

"*Es verdad,*" Carlos agreed. "Thees ees why I go weeth theem to Guadalupe Bravos. Ees no good I arrest only the leef!e feesh and leave behind the beeg one."

"Meaning Beakins, of course?"

"*Seguro que si,*" Carlos replied. "Ees same weeth me like weeth you. Eef I do not e-take all of theem at once, I weel have my job to do twice. And you are know so well as do I what moost be done wheen a *prisionero* escape."

"We go after him and bring him back," Longarm said.

"*Exactamente.* So, I most breeng een these four *bandidos* here," Carlos said. "And I have learn enough about theem now to arrest theem. Eef you help me to take theem to jail een Ciudad Jaurez, theen I weel go weeth you to Chihuahua and we weel find thees other *fugitivo,* the one who you have come here to take back to your country. Would eet not be a good theeng for us together to work?"

"Why, it'd be the smartest thing we could do, Carlos. I been doing a lot of thinking about the way I'm going to get that damn Thad Miller back to El Paso after I catch him."

"I weel promise that the *rurales* do not try and estop you from taking heem across the border weeth you," Carlos said.

Longarm nodded. "I'd a sight rather be going after him with your outfit on my side than just tearing out after him blind-eyed. We got to be careful, though, and not let these fellows here tumble to what we're up to."

While Longarm was talking, Carlos had been restoring his belt to its proper place, where his badge would be hidden. He then said, "Thees we do not need to worry over. Together we weel work een *tranquilidad*."

"Oh, sure. That part of it don't bother me a bit. Except that whatever we aim to do about this bunch here, we better get at it right away."

"*Immediatamente,*" Carlos agreed. "We capture theem and after that we take theem to Ciudad Jaurez. Theen we go to find thees Thad Miller."

"Well, I can't see there'd be a better time than right now to make our move," Longarm went on. "I'd imagine them outlaws is right in the middle of eating, and when a man's got his mind on grub, he ain't apt to pay much mind to anything else."

"Eet is time, but we must go queekly to be weeth them, before they wonder why we are so long gone."

"I don't see that we even got much of a plan, not yet," Longarm said as they started toward the glow of the cooking fire. "But I don't reckon it's going to take us long to come up with one."

95

"There ees much time left us," Carlos agreed. "Wheen we go from Ciudad Jaurez to Chihuahua Ceety, we weel make plan."

Walking a bit apart, as strangers would, Longarm and Carlos crossed the clearing and headed for the cooking fire. It was dying down now, but there were still enough live flames flickering from the bed of coals to light up the area around it where the outlaws were hunkered down in a rough circle.

Ab Beakins and Dunlap had finished their meals and put their plates aside. Smokey and Mahan were still eating, though only a few bites remained on their tin plates. The untouched plates holding the eggs that had been cooked for Longarm and Carlos were resting close to the fire where the food would be kept warm.

"Where in hell you two been?" Beakins asked as they walked into the circle of firelight. "We wasn't polite enough to wait for you to get here before we started eating, but you're going to come out better'n you got any right to."

"Meaning there's still some grub left?" Longarm asked.

"If there is, you don't get no credit for it," Smokey replied. "This ain't no place for Johnny-come-latelies."

Beakins said, "No, you two're just lucky. By the time the fellows finished their own grub they wasn't hungry enough to tear into yours. There's your plates right by the fire, where your food'd stay hot."

"I am have trouble weeth horse, getting stone from under shoe," Carlos said quickly. "Custis ees help me."

"Well, that makes sense," Beakins nodded. "Keeping his horse ready's part of this kinda life for a man. I suppose any one of us would've done the same."

Longarm and Carlos were already making a beeline to the fire. They picked up their plates. The metal pie-tins used by the outlaws were almost too hot to handle, but by juggling them from one hand to the other both men managed to carry them a short distance from the fire.

Though they'd made no arrangement to separate, both men seemed to reach agreement at the same time. Longarm moved away from the cooking fire to the left, Carlos to the right. They put their plates on the ground a bit behind the rough circle formed by the outlaws and squatted down beside them. After a few moments of silence Beakins picked up a conversation that Longarm realized immediately must have been interrupted when he and Carlos arrived.

"Now, from what you fellows said about Guadalupe Bravos, I can't see no need of us wasting our time on it," Beakins said. "So, if that's how things stands, we better pick out someplace else for our next job."

"Someplace like where?" Dunlap asked. "We wouldn't get enough gold to fill a hollow tooth in the next town downriver, the one they call Porvenir. It ain't even as big as Guadalupe Bravos."

"You been there, have you?" Beakins asked. "Because I ain't got that far from the Island yet."

"I been through it," Dunlap replied. "But that was a while back, right after I broke outa the army jail at Fort Quitman. Fast as I could, I beelined it over across the Rio Grande where I'd be safe."

"How long ago was that?" Beakins asked.

"Hell, you oughta know," Dunlap snapped. "I told you all about that when I joined up with your bunch. You and me's been riding together riding together for two years."

"So you did," Beakins agreed. "And so we have. And got along pretty good most of the time. You know I ain't one to slap out with a quirt when a man comes out flat-footed and says what's in his mind. So you don't think this Porvenir place is big enough to bother with?"

Shaking his head, Dunlap replied, "There ain't no bank, there ain't no post office, there ain't nothing but a few little shanties. From their looks, the folks living in 'em ain't got enough to pay for fixing up their roofs to turn a heavy rain."

"There ees only one place I am theenk of that weel have the reechness we are look for," Carlos said before Beakins could speak again. "Eef we want to do beeg job, where we can e-take much gold, eet ees to Chihuahua we should go."

"Chihuahua!" Beakins exclaimed. "You mean Chihuahua City?"

"*De verdad*," Carlos said. "Ees no more far as the leetle places like Porvenir."

"Like hell it ain't!" Dunlap protested. "It'd take us the better part of a week to get there, and if we didn't kill ourselves trying to get across that damn dry desert, we'd likely kill our horses."

"Oh, it ain't all that bad," Smokey protested. "I was over a lot of that country before I got outa the army. It was when we was chasing after Cochise. Sure, it's dry, but if a man keeps his eyes peeled for barrel cactus, he'll get enough water out of 'em to make out all right."

"Thees ees true," Carlos agreed. "And ees leetle water holes now and again."

"Well, I got to admit I don't know all that much about it," Beakins said. "But if you fellows ain't afeared to put your money where your mouth is, it don't sound like too bad of an idee to me."

"What you got to do in that desert country is travel nights," Smokey said. "And was I you, Ab, I'd think on it real good. There's bound to be lots of money there, but the last time I was there it was growing into a pretty sizable place."

"Ees not bigger as El Paso," Carlos added. "But ees have more banks, mebbeso more money."

"It looks to me like you men've been doing my thinking for me," Beakins told them. From the tone of his voice he was neither angry nor pleased. "I never was in Chihuahua City myself, but from what I heard, it's a pretty sizable place. Ain't there likely to be a lot of *rurales* and some local law hanging around in a town that size?"

"Why, hell, Ab, we ain't never let no local law keep us from doing pretty much what we pleased while we was waiting in some town to pull a job," Mahan said. "And the lawmen in Chihuahua City's just like they is anyplace else. They put their pants on one leg at a time."

Longarm had been listening to the outlaws, trying to keep in the background and make himself as inconspicuous as possible while they discussed their next move. Now he decided to churn the water a bit, for he could see that it would be to his advantage and to Carlos's as well to travel with a group of outlaws to Chihuahua.

He had no sources there to lead him quickly to the hideouts favored by outlaws on the run and guarantee his acceptance, and in Chihuahua Carlos would readily be recognized as a *rurale*. On the other hand, arriving in Chihuahua with an outlaw gang would give him immediate entry into the criminal circles. That wedge could shorten the search for Thad Miller by days, perhaps even by weeks. Longarm decided at once that the time had arrived for him to speak up.

"I ain't really got no business horning in," he said. "But ever since I got to the Island here I been thinking about that bunch of lawmen up at El Paso."

"Just what d'you mean, thinking about 'em?" Beakins asked, a challenge in the tone of his voice rather than his words.

"Like I told you," Longarm answered. "They was all riled up about that young outlaw that got away from 'em."

"Hell, them lawmen gets mad as a bunch of wet hens every time one of us puts something over on 'em," Beakins said.

"Sure they do," Longarm agreed. "But it wouldn't surprise me none if they ain't getting ready to come down here with a pretty good-sized posse soon as they can put one together."

"That won't bother us one damn bit," Beakins snorted. "We just fade into the brush or cross the Island and get on what we're sure is the Mexican side of the river. After them El Paso lawmen poke around a while and don't turn none of us up, they go back home."

"But how many times do they bring a company or two of soldiers from Fort Bliss along with 'em to beat the bushes?" Longarm asked. "From what I've heard, them soldiers don't pay much mind to which side of the Rio Grande they happen to be on."

100

"Now, where in the hell did you get that idea, Custis?" Beakins asked. "There never has been a time when the army got turned loose to mess into things here on the Island."

"Why, it's just saloon talk I heard while I was in El Paso on my way here," Longarm replied. "But as often as not that's the way a man's likely to hear about things."

"Was I you, I wouldn't worry too much about soldiers, Ab," Smokey put in. "I'd be putting my mind on what old Victorio's up to in that stretch of country we'd have to be crossing to get to Chihuahua City."

"Meaning what?" Beakins asked.

"Meaning I heard some talk in that *cantina* down in Guadalupe Bravos while we was there," Smokey answered. "One of them was jabbering with another one about how he kept hoping Victorio and them murdering Apaches of his wasn't gonna get no closer to the river than he is now."

"How come me and Dunlap didn't hear it the same as you did?" Mahan asked.

"Because you and him was too busy makin' love with them women when you wasn't setting in the chair in that stinkin' barbershop, trying to be made pritty," Smokey retorted tartly. "I was smart enough to be in the cantina catching up on the drinks I'd missed when we run outa liquor here."

Beakins turned to Smokey and spoke up. "Never mind who was or wasn't doing what. Just get on with whatever it is you're trying to tell us."

Nodding, Smokey continued. "Now, I wasn't thinking about it a whole lot right then, down in Guadalupe Bravos, but it just popped back into my mind when Custis said what he did a minute ago. I don't talk Mescin all that good, but I caught the general drift of what them fellows in the bar was saying."

"Well, damn it, what was it they was saying?" Beakins asked. This time his voice was sharper and less patient.

"They was talking about hearing that Victorio and his renegade Apaches was likely going to settle someplace between the Rio Grande and Chihuahua City," Smokey replied. "That'd be in them badlands where it's likely nobody was going to take the trouble it'd be getting to 'em."

"Now, that sounds just about like what Victorio'd be smart enough to do," Longarm commented. "If him and that bunch of Apaches gets a toehold on that stretch of Mexico, there ain't going to be nobody wanting to cut through it. But the way I see this thing is that Victorio ain't about to settle down no place between the Rio Grande and Chihuahua City till after he gets rid of them Paquiamis that claims most of that land now."

"Hell, there ain't enough of them Paquiamis left to give Victorio much trouble," Beakins said. "He'll chomp on 'em a while and spit out what's left, just about like you would a chaw of tobacco."

"That's right," Mahan agreed. "And if we're going to go and make a cleanup at Chihuahua City, I'd say we better hike our tails up and get over there quick as we can."

"Now, I'll put in with that," Dunlap said quickly. "If we get there pretty fast and hold our water long enough to let the Mexicans and Indians start fighting, we'll be in a prime place to make a real cleanup."

"What Dunlap's getting at sure sounds like something

102

to me," Smokey said. "Iffen the *rurales* is going to be busy with Victorio and his Apaches, we don't have to worry about the *rurales* spending much time getting after us. We can be doing what we like instead of ducking around and playing squat tag with 'em the way it's been here a time or two."

"I'll sure go along with Smokey," Mahan told the group. "I say we do it."

"What's the matter with you and Smokey?" Beakins asked Mahan. "You two act like it was you-all running things here."

"Now, don't go getting your bowels in no uproar, Ab," Mahan said. "Me and Smokey's just been talking like any man of us has got a right to do."

Even though Longarm was well aware of his status as an outsider who had not yet done anything to earn his affiliation with the gang, he saw that someone had to put a brake on what could quickly develop into trouble and spoil his chances.

"Now, I wasn't aiming to start some kind of fussing between you men," he said quickly. "I ain't got no right to butt in on what you're figuring to do, and I don't claim none. Maybe I just better move along and take my own chances by myself."

"Hold on, Custis!" Beakins said. "You been on the prod long enough to know that no outfit like this don't settle on something till everybody in it's had a chance to chew things over."

"Sure," Longarm said. "But I ain't been asked to join up with you, so I don't feel like I'd be doing the right thing by you was I just to hang around. That ain't my style at all."

103

"Hell, we already know that!" Dunlap said. "But if we do go on to Chihuahua and set up to do what we been talking about, I'd feel better with you being along instead of trying to find another man or two there."

Carlos had been silent until now, and Longarm understood the reason why. Now the undercover *rurale* spoke for the first time. "Eet ees not for me to esay what we do," he said. He was looking at Longarm as he spoke, but Longarm knew that Carlos's words were intended for the group as he went on. "Eef we are to need more men, I am better to see you weeth us than some estranger we find een Ciudad Chihuahua."

"That makes good sense to me too," Mahan said. "How d'you feel about it, Smokey?"

"Why, Custis is as good a man as I'd like to stand up alongside of," Smokey replied unhesitatingly.

"You already know my feelings," Dunlap chimed in. He was looking at Beakins as he spoke.

"Now just hold your water a minute or two," Beakins said. "I ain't forgetting nothing, damn it! I had all the chances I need to see what kind of man Custis is, but I wanted to talk private to all of you before I said anything to him about joining up with us. It seems like you've beat me to the draw, and that don't happen real often." He turned to Longarm. "I guess you're with us now, Custis. That is, if you wanta be, of course."

"Why, I reckon I'd be a plumb damn fool if I didn't," Longarm replied to them all. "I been lone-wolfing it quite a spell, and a man needs some company once in a while. I just got one question to ask Ab." Turning to Beakins, he said, "How long you reckon it'll take before we can get started for Chihuahua City?"

Chapter 9

"I don't figure it'll be much longer before Ab says it's time for us to stop and rest the horses," Longarm said as he reined in beside Carlos. When Carlos had stopped, the undercover *rurale* had not waved to him to indicate his intention to rest their horses for a moment or two. Longarm went on. "When Ab made us split up so's we wouldn't leave a big trail for somebody to pick up, he didn't let on that he wasn't going to get no time to rest our butts."

"He ees always thees way wheen gang moves," Carlos said. "He ees esay so much longer we travel, so much queeker we are get to where we go."

"You wouldn't hear me bellyaching if there was any reason for us to be hurrying," Longarm said. "Unless he's got some sorta idea about a job for the gang, or maybe he's in a rush to meet up with somebody in Chihuahua City."

When Longarm decided that Carlos was not going to reply immediately, he continued "That sun's gone on way past noontime now, and we been on the move pretty steady since daybreak. I figure that's long enough to make a man feel sorta like he needs to rein in and eat a bite and maybe even catch a little shut-eye afterwards."

"Weeth what you esay I don' not disagree," Carlos replied at last as he pulled up his horse. Without turning his eyes away from the hills that were beginning to rise above the rim of the horizon, he said, "But I am theenk eet weel be dark before the time for eshut-eye comes. After we are reach the heels, we weel be out of Apache country."

"Them hills look like they're still a pretty good ways off," Longarm said. "And they look like they're going to be real mean on the horses. I reckon they got a name?"

Gesturing toward the triple peaks, Carlos replied, "Ees call Los Tres Castillos."

"Three Castles?" Longarm asked after cudgeling his mind a moment while he brought up his scant vocabulary of Spanish. "I don't see no castles."

"Ah, but man who name theem do." Carlos smiled. "You look, you esee."

When Longarm turned to gaze in the direction of Carlos's gesture he was surprised to see that the hills might earn the fanciful name after all. To his eyes, accustomed to the imposing mountains around Denver, they remained only hills, low brown slopes which had seemed to be retreating from the outlaws since they'd first come into sight. The three low peaks humped along the western horizon in a jagged uneven line that gave promise that they might mark the end of the arid expanse of the Sonoran Desert. But now they seemed to be far out of reach.

Longarm and Carlos had pulled up in one of the few large expanses of cleared ground that they'd encountered since their before-dawn departure from a waterless overnight camp. Two days before, when they and the outlaws had splashed across the river and started riding west, the vista ahead of them had been rolling prairie, where grass grew belly-deep.

They'd made good progress over the level expanse, but the strip of green had proved to be a narrow one. They'd covered only a few miles when the big patches of grass thinned; then its greenery vanished completely as the ground rose and began to slant upward. Beyond that point there were few spots of green. Not only grass, but other vegetation as well virtually disappeared.

As they progressed, the terrain between them and the hills leveled off and became a broad sweep of rolling land that made travel easy once more. On the first days of their ride they'd traveled across the rising barren land that stretched as far ahead as the riders could see. For the next two days they'd followed the course of a brooklet, its sluggish current flowing in the opposite direction from that in which they were travelling, away from them, toward the Rio Grande.

Now, as they neared the end of their fifth day of almost constant riding, the little stream had been left far behind. The land itself had changed from rich brown loam dotted with big patches of straggled grassland. They were traveling now over an area where the lighter hue of sandy earth predominated. Here the wiry thin strands of ocotillo vied for room with closely spaced prickly-pear cactus clumps on soil that had steadily grown harder, more barren, and lighter in color. Beyond the seemingly endless stretch of gently rising terrain, the hills rose above the heat-haze to form a jagged mountainous horizon.

Turning back to Carlos, Longarm saw that his companion was no longer gazing at the mountain range. Carlos had turned to look at the maze of cactus plants that still stretched in an unbroken line between them and the mountain range.

"You see something interesting?" Longarm asked after waiting several moments for a reply to his first remarks.

"Een that direction, I theenk I am hear horses move," Carlos said as he gestured toward the horizon.

Now Longarm turned his own attention to the direction the *rurale* was watching. From one end of the jagged landscape to the other, Longarm could not see anything moving. The only growing things that met his eyes in the long vista ahead was a thick growth of tall twisted cholla cactus plants, their limbs all seeming to lean at a different angle above the stretch of ocher-hued earth.

As far as Longarm could see, the arid soil was dotted with the cactus's gnarled and faded brownish-green stalks, topped by thick-ridged light-green ferociously spiked arms. Many of them rose higher than the heads of the riders. The cactus plants were the kind that Carlos had told Longarm were called "jumping cholla" by those familiar with the area's scanty vegetation.

Earlier, when they'd first reached the edge of the cactus thicket, Ab Beakins had insisted that the group split into pairs and ride apart, to attract less attention than would a band of men passing through the pathless area. As Longarm and Carlos cut away from the others, the undercover *rurale* had cautioned Longarm to give the cactus plenty of room and to stay away as far as possible from the spikes which sprouted from the thick curving arms.

They continued riding steadily through a spread of cactus so wide and thick that it seemed endless. The plants grew in large patches or clumps and looked like deformed trees in an insane forest. Some of the stands they'd passed covered only a few yards of the arid soil, but in other places, such as the one in which they now found themselves, the cactus spread over an area of several miles.

Carlos broke the silence again. "Thees time I am to know for positive I esee sometheeng move ahead. What ees move I cannot be sure, I do not get good look."

"You're doing better'n me, then," Longarm told him. "I still ain't seen a thing new since we rode into this damn thick cactus patch."

"Ees first theeng I see seence we come to desert country," Carlos said. Without releasing the reins, he stood up in his stirrups and began surveying the area ahead of them. After a moment of squinting he went on. "I am not so tall as you, Longarm. Maybeso eef you stand up een stirrups you see more."

Longarm reined in his horse, took a turn around his saddlehorn with the reins, and stood up in his stirrups. His first quick scanning of the area around them showed no sign of anything moving at first. Then as he kept looking around, trying to twist his head sidewise to get a better view through the maze of the cactus's spreading arms, he saw at one side the bobbing hat crowns of two of their outlaw companions. He could not identify them because he could only catch an occasional glimpse of a hat or a horse's rump through the dense stands of the all-prevailing cholla cactus.

When he swiveled around as far as possible, trying to get a glimpse of the others in their group, Longarm saw nothing except the high twisted tapering tips of cholla branches. He was getting ready to lower himself to his saddle again when he spotted Ab Beakins and Mahan emerging from one of the thick clumps of the screening cactus.

"There's Ab Beakins and Mahan over yonder, not too far off," he told Carlos. "And I reckon them two hats I see over in the other direction is bound to be Dunlap and Smokey, even if all I can make out is the tops of their hats. These cactus stands is so thick that it's downright hard to tell who anybody is."

"They were not in front from us, the others?" Carlos asked.

"More sideways than in front," Longarm replied. Then he frowned as he belatedly recognized the significance of Carlos's words. He shook his head. "I ain't even smart as a fresh-dropped colt today. What I been looking at has got to mean that what you seen or heard right up ahead is somebody besides them."

"Thees I theenk ees true," Carlos said. "Indios. Maybe so Victorio, maybeso not."

Longarm had just reached the same conclusion. "You figure the redskins is just skulking along? Ain't it more'n likely they're getting ready to jump us?"

Carlos shrugged. "*Como sí, como sa*. There ees but one way to find out."

"Meaning we go right on along the way we been traveling?"

"Thees ees the way that take us to Chihuahua Ceety, and to there is where we weesh to go, no?"

"Oh, I ain't argufying with you, Carlos, and I sure ain't saying we oughta do anything except push on ahead. But what about them outlaw redskins?"

"Eef we meet Victorio and hees Apaches, all guns we got we weel need. You, me, the outlaws too. Ees real bad Indio, thees Victorio."

"You don't have to tell me that. I already know it. I seen the wanted posters that went out on him when he broke away from the Mimbres reservation on our side of the Rio Grande," Longarm replied. "Is what you're try-ing to say right now that we're on his stamping ground?"

"Eef what you are call hees estamp ground ees where he make village, eet is to north from here. But Victorio ees *astuto,* he ees make one village here, one more there, maybe still other one een different place."

"If that's the way of it, then we better keep our eyes peeled."

"*De seguro,*" Carlos agreed. "Victorio ees move like he please to. Even us of the *rurales* cannot know where he ees until he make the attack—" Carlos stopped short as the crack of a shot, then another, and finally a quick scatter of gunfire broke the desert stillness.

"Looks like we been speaking of the devil," Longarm said.

He rose in his stirrups to get a better view of the ter-rain. All that he could see ahead was a wisp of yellowish powder smoke rising above the tops of the spiny cactus. As he dropped back into his saddle another distant shot rang out, and it was followed by a brief rattle of random shooting.

"Six or eight guns," Longarm said as the crackle of the volleyed shots died away. "I'd say some of them outlaws up ahead of us has stepped into a wasp nest."

"We do not have choice but to help," Carlos said.

As he spoke he was reining his mount in the direction from which the shots had sounded. Longarm jerked the reins of his own horse to follow Carlos. Ahead of them they could now see thin threads of powder smoke staining the windless blue sky as they strung above the cactus.

Carlos pointed toward the yellowish fumes. "Ees there the Indios," he said. "They use the old guns that are make beeg smoke."

"But their bullets takes down a man as fast as the ones from new guns," Longarm replied with a mirthless smile. "Mebbe they don't carry as far, but they'll kill you just as dead if they hit the right spot."

"*Es verdad*," Carlos agreed. "We must get weeth others so fast as we can. Eef together we surprise Apaches from behind we maybeso have best chance against theem."

"If it ain't too big of a bunch, we just might," Longarm said. "But this damn cactus sure don't give a man much room to go zigzagging around in."

Longarm and Carlos were now close enough to hear an occasional yell during intervals between the intermittent gunfire. The distance was still too great for them to catch the words, and half the time they could not distinguish between the shouts from the outlaws and those of the Apaches.

Without speaking further, they reined their horses into a slanting course that would take them to the edge of the area where the gunfire was sounding. As they progressed, the firing became even more sporadic. The indi-

112

vidual shots were coming at longer and longer intervals, and there were also fewer war cries from the Apaches.

"Eet seems to me I am not so many guns hear now," Carlos said after they'd been riding for only a short time.

"I was thinking the same thing myself," Longarm said. "Either somebody's running now or—" He did not finish his remark, but shook his head.

Suddenly a bullet whistled past Longarm's head. Its whining passage and the report of the gun which had fired it were the first indications that he and Carlos were reaching the heart of the danger zone. They'd been riding side by side, as close together as the crowded stands of thick cactus stalks would allow. Now Longarm gestured to Carlos by stretching his arm and bringing it around in a sweeping half circle to indicate that their strategy should now be to split up and attack the Apaches from different angles.

Carlos understood the gesture at once. He nodded and began veering away. Longarm had been riding on Carlos's left side. He twitched the reins to wheel his horse, and rode at a slant to circle around toward the Indians from the opposite direction. He'd just gotten close enough to be within pistol range as well as rifle range when his eyes caught a flick of motion between the cactus stalks.

When the Apache rider came in sight, Longarm was ready. He triggered a rifle shot and the bullet went true. The Apache had not yet raised his rifle when Longarm's slug drove home. The redskin's body jerked backward and toppled from the horse. Longarm did not waste time going to take a closer look at the fallen Indian; he knew that his aim had been good.

There was another Apache visible by now, starting toward him. Longarm brought up his rifle again, but before he could shoulder it the crack of Carlos's gun broke the air, and the Indian who'd been galloping toward him fell forward on the neck of his horse. The dead man lay along the animal's spine for a moment before the horse veered and the corpse pitched to the ground.

Even though the encounter between Longarm and Carlos and the two attacking Indians had lasted only a few moments, the firing from the Apaches ahead had now become even more sporadic. Their war cries had diminished, but the few wild shouts and the almost constant shots that cracked through the cactus stalks gave Longarm and Carlos the guidance they needed.

As he rode, Longarm twisted to reach his saddlebags and groped for a supply of fresh shells. He thumbed the cartridges into the rifle's loading-port until it would hold no more, and dropped the remainder of the ammunition into his pocket. Just when he was sure that he'd have his Winchester fully loaded with the shells he needed to allow him to hold his own through what gave signs of being a long-running fight, another volley of shots broke the air ahead of them.

For a moment the gunfire was so heavy and the shots so close together that Longarm had trouble distinguishing between the sharp crackling reports of the outlaws' late-model high-powered rifles and the flatter blasts of the older guns of the Apaches.

Glancing toward the position Carlos had occupied, he was surprised to see that his companion was galloping away from him. Reining his horse around, Longarm spurred his horse and followed. Carlos was just disappearing into a sprawling cactus thicket that rose just ahead of them.

By the time Longarm reached the edge of the dense growth Carlos had disappeared, and the rifle fire beyond the cactus stand that had been so heavy for a moment was diminishing. Pushing into the tricky patch of spiny growth, Longarm had no choice but to abandon the idea of trying to stay close to the *rurale*, but he satisfied himself with the steady gait his horse was maintaining through the tangle.

He'd gone only a short distance when he saw the first body sprawled on the ground. It was an Indian, and Longarm did not rein in, for a glance ahead revealed a second lifeless form. Mahan's face was upturned, a reddish-black dot in his forehead and widespread eyelids giving him the appearance of having three eyes.

Longarm saw at once that there was nothing he could do to help the dead man, and did not rein in. Even before he'd reached the third corpse he recognized it as being an Indian, and passed it as he'd passed Mahan's body, without hesitating. Smokey's body was a dozen or more yards deeper in the thicket. The dead man lay in a kneeling huddle, his chin almost touching his knees, his revolver lying beside an open outstretched hand. Almost within reach of the pistol the body of an Apache sprawled across the Indian's rifle.

Longarm moved steadily ahead. There was no noise ahead now except for the distant thunks made by the hooves of Carlos's horse. Here the treelike cholla cactus grew thicker, as did the ground-hugging cow's tongue with its inch-long needles. Longarm's horse began high-stepping, whinnying now and then when the needles on the clump of the low-growing cow's tongue plants drove through even its thick hide.

Two dead Apache warriors lay crossways, one atop the other, only a yard away from the bodies of Dunlap and Ab Beakins. The Indians were on one side of the tall spiny arms of a cholla cactus, the bodies of the outlaws on the other. The treelike bottom of the cholla had been almost demolished by the shots that had torn into its tree-like trunk.

Longarm started to rein in, but the burst of gunfire that sounded ahead changed his mind. He toed his horse's belly, and restrained his impatience as another spatter of shots broke the air. In spite of his efforts to get the horse moving at a faster gait, the animal moved only slightly faster, forced as it was to pick its way between the twisted trunks of the warped, slanting cholla.

Fighting his impatience, Longarm kept up the best pace possible until the cactus stalks thinned at the edge of the clump and he could see Carlos standing beside the twitching, leg-thrashing form of his prone horse. Blood was seeping in a steady flow from the downed animal's throat.

Carlos sill held his rifle shouldered, his head slanted as he sighted while swinging the weapon's muzzle, trying to get another shot at the now-distant Apache. The Indian was bending low on the back of his galloping mount as it continued to carry him across the high-grassed expanse of open prairie beyond the cactus clump.

Carlos triggered off his shot, but the bullet did nothing more than raise a small spurt of dust between the legs of the galloping animal. Working the Winchester's lever in its awkward position with the rifle still shouldered,

Carlos fired again. This shot was no more accurate than the first.

As he turned to follow the fleeing Apache's course, Carlos saw Longarm for the first time. He chopped the air with his right hand, signaling Longarm to follow the Apache. Longarm nodded and dug his heels into his horse's flank.

Chapter 10

After the many miles his horse had been ridden since daybreak, Longarm knew that the animal was very tired. He could gauge its weariness by the sluggish way it responded to the drumming of his boot heels on its sides. Then he realized that the fleeing Apache's mount was making no better progress than his own, and that he now had a good chance of overtaking the Indian.

Longarm shifted his grip on the Winchester, grasping it now with his right hand by the throat of the stock to leave his left hand free for the reins. Now he could still control his horse, and it was not the first time he'd handled the rifle as though it were a pistol. He was ready to bring the weapon into immediate action as soon as he was close enough to his fleeing quarry. Ahead of him, he could see the Apache drumming the heels of his moccasined feet on his horse's belly.

Longarm's wait turned out to be a short one. In spite of the Indian's efforts to speed its pace, the Apache's mount stumbled and its stride faltered. Then the animal recovered, and it began galloping again, but the faster pace lasted only a few minutes. Now Longarm began to gain ground slowly, for though his own horse was still faltering, the one ridden by the Apache was now moving even more slowly. But the chase seemed much longer to Longarm than it was in reality, for the minutes ticked away without really shrinking the gap of almost a mile that still separated him from the Apache.

Longarm kept on in his dogged effort to get within rifle range of the running redskin, but they'd already covered a great deal of ground and the distance between them still remained too great. Then when Longarm glanced ahead again, he saw that the Apache had reached a long steep ridge, and though his quarry was approaching the rising slope in a long slant that would ease the strain of the horse in mounting it, Longarm saw his chance to close the gap.

While the Apache was urging his tiring horse up the slope, Longarm reined his mount to follow the base of the rise. On level ground, with the Apache moving much slower than he had at the beginning of the chase, Longarm at last got close enough to let off a telling shot. He reined in and got the Apache in the sights of his rifle just as the redskin was silhouetted on the crest.

Longarm squeezed off a shot. The Apache's body jerked and he threw up his arms, but stayed in the saddle. Longarm pumped the Winchester's loading lever and slammed it home; now he took quick aim and sent a second rifle slug after the first. This time the Apache sagged and fell from his horse. He dropped just as the animal had topped the ridge, and the Indian's limp form slid down the opposite side of the crest and disappeared.

With a victory almost won, Longarm wasted no time in reining his mount straight up the steep slope. He reached its top and looked down into the little semi-circular valley below. The Apache he'd snapshotted was lying sprawled and still, near the bottom of the bowl-like valley's rise. Raising his eyes, he saw something else as well. Beyond the base of the long curving upslope there were a half-dozen conical buffalo-hide tipis of an Apache village.

Longarm started his horse down the slope and rode toward the tipis. He kept his eyes fixed on the tipis, but no Apaches came out of any of them. He'd covered most of the half-mile expanse of prairie that lay between him and the village when from behind the shelter of a ridged line of the broken earth where he'd been lurking an Apache warrior leaped to his feet. He did not have a rifle, but as he loosed a howling war cry and started running toward Longarm, he drew a wickedly long knife from a belt-sheath. Longarm lowered the muzzle of his Winchester, handling it as though it were a pistol, and stopped the Indian's charge with a single shot.

Reining in as the Apache warrior fell, Longarm locked a knee around his saddlehorn and sat examining the terrain. The Indian he'd been chasing still lay huddled at the spot where he'd fallen from his mount. Between the moments when Longarm shifted his attention from one area of the valley to another, he flicked quick glances at the tipis in the event that another Apache warrior might be lurking in the seemingly deserted village.

Longarm stretched his legs by standing up in the stirrups. The added height gave him a better view of the little bowl-like valley, and he was beginning to feel relieved that the Indian camp showed no signs of life when a man burst from the flaps of one of the conical shelters. He glanced for only a split-second at Longarm, then turned and started to run around the base of the conical shelter, but before he turned Longarm had gotten a glimpse of his white face and white hands.

Longarm's reaction was immediate and automatic. He realized at once that any white man trying to escape from an Apache tipi must be a prisoner seeking freedom. Gathering the reins of his mount and jerking them around, he dug his heels into the weary animal's flanks and headed for the tipis. The escaping man was already running, but when he heard the thudding hooves of Longarm's galloping horse getting close to him he glanced around and put on a fresh burst of speed.

"Grab my pommel and swing up!" Longarm shouted above the thudding of his horse's drumming hoofbeats as he reached the running man.

He yanked at the reins and the horse tried valiantly to stop, but only succeeded in slowing down a bit. Longarm felt the running man's hands brush along his back as the fugitive grabbed for the pommel. Then the saddle slipped a fraction of an inch, and the horse snorted and tried to rear as the man pulled himself up to its rump.

"Go on!" the man said. His lips were so close to Longarm's ear that his voice sounded like a shout. "I'll hang on!"

Glancing at the row of tipis, Longarm saw no sign that anyone was stirring around them, but even so, his decision to rejoin Carlos without any further delay was made in an instant. Reining his tiring horse around, he prodded it hard with his boot toe. As the steed picked up its pace, the man he'd rescued spoke again.

"Hey, you're going back to where them redskins are!" he said. "I figured—"

"Whatever you figured, you're wrong," Longarm snapped over his shoulder. "There's a man over that rise, one I'm riding with, and for all I know he might still be in trouble. You just hold on and stay quiet till I find out what's happening on the other side of this hump."

During the few moments needed for the horse to return to the top of the ridge's inner rim, the man behind Longarm was silent. Longarm heard no more shots from the opposite side of the high curving earthen embankment. He could not decide whether the stillness was a good sign or a bad one until he reached the rim. At last the exhausted horse topped the slope and Longarm reined in. Raising himself in his stirrups, he glanced down.

Carlos was standing alone a few dozen yards beyond the spot where Longarm had last seen him. His rifle dangled from his hand. Beyond, at the edge of the thicket as well as on the open ground between it and the base of the rise, the motionless forms of four Apaches were sprawled on the ground, two on each side of the creek bed's banks. Longarm toed his horse ahead. It stiffened its legs and half walked, half slid down the slope.

"It don't seem to me you had much more trouble than I did," Longarm said as he reined in a few feet from the *rurale*. As he spoke Longarm took out a cigar and flicked a match into flame with his thumbnail.

"For more of eets kind, I do not weesh soon," Carlos replied. His eyes were fixed on the man who sat on the horse's rump. "I am hear you eshoot on other side of ridge. You are have more trouble as I do, no?"

"Maybe so, maybe no," Longarm answered through the cloud of smoke that now veiled his face. "I'll say this much, it'd've been a real hot time if there'd been more of them Apaches."

"But for the fight we make, you have sometheeng to eshow," Carlos noted. "I see you are capture thees Thad Miller you come to the Island to find."

"Now, hold on!" the man on the horse's rump protested. "Whoever it is you said I was, my name ain't Thad Miller!"

"You are e-lie!" Carlos snapped. "You I know, maybe better as you know me! I have see you een camp on Island, I am go weeth you to Guadalupe Bravos! Wheen I do thees, you theenk I am outlaw like as you, but I am *rurale! Seguro que si,* I am e-know you."

While Carlos was speaking, Longarm had felt the involuntary muscle-twitching of the man on his horse's rump and swept his hand to the butt of his Colt. He did not draw, certain that if Miller had a gun, he would have used it on the Apache from whom he'd been running.

From the moment Miller had first spoken, Longarm had realized that he was no fool. In the present situation he was positive that his prisoner would behave, gambling even against high odds that he would have an opportunity to escape, as he'd done so often before.

Twisting in the saddle, Longarm said, "Well?" When he got no reply, he went on. "Now, you heard what my friend there said. I ain't an unreasonable man, but the next time you open your mouth it better be to tell me the truth."

Carlos broke in, his voice carrying assurance as he told Longarm, "Eef I am not sure who thees one ees, I do not esay hees name."

"Well, now!" Longarm exclaimed when the man on the horse's rump remained silent. Speaking over his shoulder, he said, "Seeing as I've found out who you are, I got to tell you who I am. My name's Custis Long, and I'm a deputy United States marshal outa the Denver office. I come all the way here from there to take you back with me, and that's what I aim to do."

"You're the marshal they call Longarm?" Miller asked.

"That's right."

"Then you got no right to arrest me, damn it! Your badge ain't worth a cow turd in Mexico!"

"Why, I don't need to tell you I've done arrested you, Miller. And don't even try telling me lies," Longarm said. His voice was level and he spoke in a soft conversational tone, but no one hearing it would have any doubt of the steel that was also in his words. "Even if I didn't know better, the law here in Mexico gives us Federal marshals the same rights the *rurales* has when they come into the U.S. on a case."

"*Seguro que si*," Carlos said. He smiled, a flick of his lips. "Eef you feel ees better, I arrest you myself and go weeth my fren Longarm to border. Theen I surrender you to heem there."

"Like hell you'll arrest me!" Miller snapped. "You think I don't know about what you greasers call *la ley del fuego*? If I let you get me outa sight of this American lawman, you'd put a bullet in my back and say you had to shoot me because I was trying to escape! I'll take

125

my chances with a U.S. marshal any day of the week sooner'n I would with you."

"I reckon you figure I'll take that as a compliment, but I don't," Longarm said. He paused for a moment, frowning. "I got a question that's been nibbling at me ever since Carlos told me who you was."

"Go on and ask it, then," Miller told him. "But I ain't going to swear I'll give you any kinda answer."

"What in hell was you doing in that Apache camp?" Longarm asked. "Figuring to throw in with Victorio?"

"Now, that'd be the last thing I'd do! No, them redskins jumped me and caught me while I was going from that litle old dinky town down south of the Island, heading for Chihuahua City. Taken my gun and everything else I had. From what I could make out they was aiming to do some kinda dance around me, and I know enough about Apaches to know they'd kill me."

"Ees too bad they do not," Carlos said unsympathetically.

"Don't worry about that," Longarm said. "I'm just glad to find out I nabbed the right man. Maybe I didn't think to mention it before, but I never had set eyes on this fellow here before I left on the job I come down here to do."

"Theen een Los Estados Unidos you are not yourself to arrest heem?"

"Now, you ain't forgetting what I told you on the Island, are you?" Longarm asked. "Or maybe I didn't mention it then, when you and me talked the first time, after you'd got back from that place he went to with you on the Rio Grande. But till I seen him a few minutes ago, I didn't know him from Adam's off-ox."

126

"Eef I forget before, I remember now," Carlos said. "But thees ees one you want. I am know heem, he ees look like hees father, and heem I am know too."

"That'd be Clell Miller, the gunslinger in El Paso?"

"*Sí*," Carlos said.. "Clell he ees dead, but thees son from heem is as bad like father."

"Looks like we done our job, then," Longarm said. "And since that's the way of it, we better quit jawing and start moving before any more of Victorio's men shows up."

"There ees first one theeng we must do," Carlos said.

"And what might that be?" Longarm asked.

"*Los bandidos*," Carlos replied. "Those from Island. We most see they are bury. Eet ees true they are not good meen, but are *Cristianos* same like you, same like me."

"I reckon you're right," Longarm agreed. Jerking his thumb toward Thad Miller, he said, "And we got just the man over there that can do the grave-digging."

"Now, hold on!" Miller protested. His face was twisted in anger. "I ain't about to do no—"

"You'll do what we tell you to!" Longarm snapped. Turning back to Carlos, he said, "I don't guess it's occurred to you that we ain't got nothing to dig graves with?"

"I have theenk of thees thing," Carlos replied. "Een desert like thees we do not deeg. We only can put dirt over theem, and branches to save theem from being tear apart by *los zopolotes*."

"I reckon that's about all we can do," Longarm agreed. "And with all of them fellows dead, we got more horses than we rightly know to do with. So we'll pick out the best one and put Miller on it."

Thad Miller opened his mouth as though to protest again, but closed it without speaking when he saw the expressions on the faces of Longarm and Carlos.

"*Beuno*," Carlos agreed. "We weel estart so soon as we are feenesh weeth the burying."

Longarm nodded. "Quick as we can get that job done, we can head for the border, and I'll be on my way back to Denver with my prisoner."

"Wheen you esay, I am ready," Carlos told him. "I also do not weesh to be here wheen other Apaches from thees camp get back."

"Well, if they do, we'll shake 'em off."

"Een such country as thees, eet weel not be easy to do like you say and eshake theem off," Carlos said. "They weel see us wheen we estart *al norte*."

"Now, we don't need to jump off of that bridge till we get to it," Longarm said.

"Jomp off from the breedge?" Carlos frowned. "*Amigo*, you most not to remember that from the Rio Grande we are many miles away."

"Oh, don't pay me no mind." Longarm smiled. "All I was doing was blabber mouthing something I picked up from my daddy when I was just a little tad in knee-britches, back in West Virginia. What it means is, let's not go looking for trouble till trouble finds us."

"Ah," Carlos said. "*Un proverbio*, no?"

"You'd call it that," Longarm agreed. "But instead of us palavering thisaway, we better be getting started."

With Carlos leading the way, Thad Miller in the center, and Longarm bringing up the rear, they started back to take care of the unpleasant task that awaited them before their longer journey began.

• • •

Ahead of Longarm and his companions the lights of Ciudad Juarez were now clearly visible. They had changed from an almost imperceptible smear on the horizon into a glow that was reflected from the sky. The change had been so gradual that they'd noticed it only now, when the glow had parted into widely separated individual gleams which now outlined the roofs of the town's buildings and were bright enough to drown the starshine behind them.

They were riding side by side, with Longarm and Carlos flanking Thad Miller. Their long ride, which now gave promise that it would soon be ended, had been largely one of silence.

For the first two days Longarm and Carlos had talked quite a bit, but Thad Miller had ridden in tight-lipped silence, not even trying to talk with either of them. During the second two days as saddle-weariness began to take its toll, the remarks exchanged between the two lawmen had been fewer and spaced more widely apart, and Miller had maintained the same stubborn refusal to speak. He'd eaten his share of their dwindling rations without saying a word, and had been equally silent during their infrequent rest stops between meals.

Since they'd set out that morning in the first light of before-sunrise dawn, they'd ridden in virtually total silence through the day's broiling heat. Now, with the long afternoon stretching behind them, their stomachs were growling as nightfall crept up to end their sixth day.

All three men knew that at noon they'd eaten the last of their trail rations, and none of them, not even Thad

Miller, had complained of being hungry. Throughout the seemingly endless hours of broiling heat as the sun slipped across a vivid blue cloudless sky, their clothing grew heavy with the sweat it had absorbed since they'd begun their ride in the before-sunrise dawn. The trail dust was clotted in small grimy patches on their dust-stained and heavily stubbled faces, and streaked with the dripping beads of sweat, for even now in the beginning hours of darkness, the heat still radiated from the ground.

Since their noonday stop, Longarm and Carlos had exchanged only a dozen or so words. Their horses, tired even before they'd set out, were now plodding as though their hooves were shod with lumps of lead.

Carlos broke the silence which had been hanging over them. "We are finally to get to Ciudad Juarez," he said to Longarm. "I e-theenk tonight we sleep een bed, and we do not keep open the one eye so prisoner ees not escape."

"I sure ain't going to be one to turn down a good bed after all them nights I had to sleep with nothing but a blanket between me and the ground," Longarm told his companion. "But if it wasn't for that new bunch of damned red tape them politicians back East has draped on us lawmen, I'd be pushing along right now across the Rio Grande to El Paso with this damn Miller."

"For thees you cannot blame us een the *rurales*," Carlos said. "We are have same trouble wheen we breeng prisoner back across reever from your country."

"Oh, it ain't nothing for me and you to argufy about," Longarm said quickly. "I reckon the *rurales* has got a good jail where I can put this prisoner so he won't get no ideas about making a getaway during the night?"

130

"So good a one as you weel find een Mexico," Carlos said. "Eet ees not far from where we are now. I weel geeve order to the *carcelero* and make esure he ees keep especial watch on heem."

"Now, I take that real kindly," Longarm replied. "And just to prove it, I'll stand the drinks soon as this Miller rascal's put away."

"I am of sorrow that I cannot go weeth you to cantina," Carlos replied. "Bot here in Ciudad Juarez ees very streect *comandante*. He ees not allow *rurales* to dreenk een cantina. Do not worry for me, Longarm. Een office of *rurales* we have small room where ees bed, I esleep there."

"Well, I sure ain't going to cross over to El Paso tonight and have to come back tomorrow to pick up this damn outlaw. You got any idea where I'd be best off for the night?"

"Ees good *posada*, El Pajaro Azul, only leetle way from *rurale* office."

"Fine," Longarm said. "That's where I'll stay then. Are you sure you ain't going to let me buy you a drink or two?"

"Ees not I do not weesh to, ees I must the orders of our *comandante* obey," Carlos said. "And do not for thees prisoner worry. I weel take of heem the best from care."

Chapter 11

Longarm walked leisurely down the street, heading for the central section of Ciudad Juarez. He'd just parted from Carlos and Thad Miller at the door of the squat cut-stone building that housed the jail and the *rurale* headquarters. He led his horse now instead of riding. After the days he'd spent in the saddle during the long ride to Ciudad Juarez, Longarm's calves and thighs were both moving stiffly.

He'd refused Carlos's offer to put his mount into the stables that were behind the building housing the *rurales*, for he knew that the horse needed to be walked, just as he badly needed to stretch his saddle-cramped legs. As he walked along, looking for the sign of the hotel Carlos had recommended, Longarm breathed a small sigh of relief when he felt his cramped muscles begin to loosen up and feel normal again.

Though the night was well advanced and many of the houses and buildings on the narrow crooked streets of the border city were dark, enough light spilled from the windows and doors of those which still showed signs of life to brighten the cobblestoned streets. An occasional wagon creaked past him, less often a buggy or two-wheeled *carreta,* and now and again he met a man leading a loaded burro or horse.

There were no streetlights in Ciudad Juarez. What little illumination the streets had came from the truncated swinging doors of the saloons and cantinas, which seemed at first glance to make up the bulk of the town's buildings. At many street intersections there was a saloon on at least two and often three or four corners. The blobs of brilliance above and below the truncated swinging doors splashed across the unpaved streets and enabled him to read the street signs, even though on most of them the painted names were faded and peeling.

Luck or chance led Longarm to look down the second or third of the intersecting streets that he crossed, and on the roof of a two-story adobe building only a dozen steps away he saw flickers of small lighted lanterns that outlined the figure of a grossly oversized bird. It was painted bright blue, and Longarm followed the clue that made him believe he'd reached his destination. Turning, he angled across to the building.

As he drew nearer, he could make out the lettering of the sign that now became visible on the simulated branch clasped by the bird's feet: *El Pajaro Azul—Cuartos con Baños y Comidos—English speaking.*

"Well, old son," Longarm muttered. "If that ain't the place Carlos told you to look out for, you've forgot all the Mexican lingo you ever learned."

Tugging at the reins of his horse, Longarm headed for the hotel. He passed by the swinging doors of the saloon that occupied one corner of the building, dismounted, and wrapped the reins of his horse around the hitch rail which stretched in front of the street-level door. It was open, and light spilled from it. Longarm reached it and stepped inside.

He felt at home immediately, for the lobby of the building could have been a twin to the dozens of small hotels in any of the towns to which his job had taken him. A half-dozen chairs and a small settee filled the space between the entrance and the registration desk at the rear of the room. Behind the desk, a small tier of pigeonholes took up all the available wallspace.

"*No habla Español,*" Longarm informed the chubby young clerk who came from a room behind the registration desk which occupied most of the lobby. "I hope that sign out there's right."

"Of course eet ees, *señor,* as you are now find out," the clerk replied. "Eet ees room you weesh, no?"

"One with a bathroom," Longarm said. "And I hope you got a place for my horse."

"We have the stable, ees een back from here. The horse weel be cared for, I am to assure you." The clerk gestured toward the registration ledger that occupied the center of the counter. "Eef you weel please esign? And you weel estay tonight only?"

"If I'm lucky, I will," Longarm replied. He dug into his pocket and produced a handful of coins. Selecting a twenty-dollar gold piece, he dropped it on the counter. "I guess this'll take care of however much I'll owe you when I leave. That'll likely be tomorrow, so I'll pick up whatever change there's left outa it then, if that suits you all right."

"Eet weel be most satisfactory, *señor,*" the clerk re-

plied. "And we are most please to have you as guest."
He turned to grope in one of the pigeonholes, took out
a key, and dropped it on the counter. "For your room.
And you weel need bath, no?"

"I need a bath worse'n I need a bed," Longarm
answered. "A good hot one, that I can soak in
awhile."

"Eet weel be soon ready, *señor*. One-quarter the hour,
mas o menos, eef thees ees to e-satisfy you." The clerk
bent in a half-bow. "You have the luggage, no?"

"Just my saddlebags," Longarm answered. "I reckon
you can get whoever takes care of my nag to bring 'em
up to my room. And I'll want my rifle along with 'em,
if it ain't too much bother."

"All weel be done as you weesh," the clerk assured
him. He gestured toward the key. "Eef I can eshow you
now to your room, eet weel be my pleasure to esee that
all else ees done as you request."

"Why, you don't need to put yourself out," Longarm
said quickly. "I reckon I can read the room numbers without no help." He glanced around to find the stairway. "I
see them stairs, I guess they're all I need to look for."

"As long as you are esatisfy, *señor,*" the clerk said.
"And permit me to weesh you a pleasant esleep."

Longarm wasted no time in climbing the stairs and
locating the number of his room in the door-lined corridor. As he inspected the numbers on the doors he
noticed that the one labeled *Baño—Bath* was almost
directly opposite his room. Unlocking his room door,
he went inside. The bed, already turned down, was the
first thing that caught his eyes.

Tossing his hat on the nearest chair, Longarm shrugged

136

out of his vest and shirt. For a moment the pitcher of water and the washbowl resting on a small stand at the end of the room drew his attention, but the thought of a hot bath in the tub across the hall popped into his mind and he shook his head.

Two long steps took him to the wide bed and he eased himself down on it. The mattress was surprisingly soft. It seemed to engulf him and welcome him. He waited only long enough to lever out of his boots; then without the need to force himself to remain awake and listen for noises in the darkness until he was positive that no danger threatened, he stretched out and for the first time in many weeks fell asleep almost at once.

When he awoke with a start, Longarm wondered first how long he'd been asleep. He knew he'd slept more deeply than usual, for while he'd been sleeping someone had placed his saddlebags on a chair just inside the door and leaned his rifle against them. Whoever had brought up his gear had not roused him, though usually any small sound close by would bring him from the soundest sleep, instantly alert.

"You got to watch out closer, old son," Longarm said into the stillness of the room. "You just ain't used to being in a foreign country. It's a good thing who-ever brought that truck upstairs was honest and friendly, because it might've been somebody that'd stepped in to cut your throat." Yawning, he stepped to the nearby chair where he'd left his vest and fished one of his long thin cigars and a match out of his vest pocket. He scratched the match into flame by flicking his iron-hard thumbnail across its head.

After he'd puffed the cigar into life he went on. "Old son, if you been sleeping longer'n a few minutes, you're going to have a cold bath instead of a good hot one, but it ain't likely you taken more'n forty winks. All the same, you better get your lazy butt outa bed and over across the hall to that bathroom so as you can start soaking away the trail grime."

Adequately, spurred into action by the thought of bathing in hot water, indoors, and in a bathtub instead of being hunkered down at the edge of a water hole, Longarm stepped to the door and opened it a crack. He peered in both directions along the corridor and saw no signs of activity.

As he closed the door and stepped away from it he added, "Late as it is, you ain't likely to run into nobody in the hall. It'll be a lot easier to get rid of everything but your long johns right here in the room, and just step across the hall in your balbriggans. There ain't a soul out there to see you, and at night thisaway there ain't the chance of a snowball in hell there'll be anybody looking when you step over there and back."

The thought of stretching out in the waiting tub of hot water gave speed to Longarm's moves. Pushing his saddlebags on the chair to the floor, he sat down long enough to peel away his socks. Then he stood up and shed his trousers.

Wearing only his long underwear now, Longarm opened the room door a crack, just wide enough for him to listen for noises in the hallway. He heard nothing, and saw nothing when he peered through the narrow slit. Opening the door wider, he slipped into the corridor, closed the door quickly, and took the two long strides needed to cross the hall.

Longarm opened the door of the bathroom and quickly closed it behind him without taking his eyes off the corridor. He froze when a small surprised gasp sounded behind him, and wheeled around instantly. His jaw dropped and his eyes popped open wide when a saw a woman sitting in the bathtub. Her hair was swathed in a knotted towel, and as Longarm stared she brought her arms up and crossed them over her bulging pink-tipped breasts in the manner of so many women who are surprised while in the nude.

After staring at Longarm for a moment in wide-eyed silence, she found her voice and said, "How dare you come in here while I'm bathing! Get out at once!"

Uncharacteristically, Longarm had lost his voice and only a stifled gargle came from his mouth when he started to speak. Clearing his throat, he tried again, and this time the words came out.

"I'm sorry as can be, ma'am," he said. "But I ordered up a good hot bath when I signed in at the desk downstairs. Then I dozed off in my room, it's right across the hall. I just figured when I woke up that my bathwater was getting cold, so I hurried in without stopping to look or even having any idea that somebody else was in here."

"Please hurry out, then!" she snapped. "I ordered a hot bath earlier this evening myself. From what you just said, my room must be next to yours, and when I heard the porter preparing the tub, I assumed that it was mine."

"Well, ma'am, I ain't going to argufy with you," Longarm told her. "It won't be no trouble to get the tub filled fresh when you're finished. I'll just—"

He started to open the door, but before he'd done more than crack it, the sound of laughter and high-pitched voices came in from the corridor. Without opening the door further, Longarm peered through the crack between it and the frame.

He saw three or four people, at least two women and two men, standing in the hallway in front of one of the doors a short distance down the hall. The group showed no signs that they intended to move in the immediate future. Instead, they began talking again. Their words were only garbled sounds, but their laughter carried well.

Longarm closed the door quickly and turned back to the woman in the tub. He saw that she had let her arms fall after he turned to leave. Now he got a quick glimpse of her full firm breasts, their bright pink rosettes beginning to bud. She folded her arms again, but even the quick glimpse he'd gotten was having its effect on Longarm. After being in a womanless world for so many weeks, his groin had started stirring and he could feel himself beginning an erection. He realized that the woman in the tub had noticed the bulging at his crotch as she folded her arms again.

"I ain't staying here just to annoy you, ma'am," he told her. "There's a bunch of people out there in the hall, and I'd have to shove through 'em to get to the door of my room. I ain't exactly dressed for that."

"You're better dressed than I am," she retorted. "And I'm certainly not going to leave this bathtub."

"I ain't asked you to do that," Longarm assured her. "But seeing a pretty lady like you does things to a man."

"So I have noticed. But I—" She broke off quickly before finishing what she'd started to say.

"Now, that's just something a man can't help," Longarm said. He was floundering for the words he needed to frame an apology that would not call any additional attention to the bulge which was now fully outlined and pushing against the fabric of his underwear.

"Oh, I can understand that—" She broke off again, but did not take her eyes off him.

"Maybe the best thing for me to do is turn around," Longarm said. "You see, I been out in the desert for a spell, and seeing such a pretty lady as you are—" As he spoke he was swiveling to put his back to her. Over his shoulder, he asked, "Is that better?"

A long moment passed before the woman in the tub replied, "I think—" She stopped for a moment before going on. "I think I liked what I was looking at a minute ago better than what I'm seeing now. And having to twist your head that way when you talk certainly can't be very comfortable. Why don't you turn this way again?"

Longarm had turned his head away from her to ease the strain on his neck muscles. He heard the water in the bathtub splashing, and swiveled around. The woman in the tub had gotten to her feet. Her smooth white skin was wet and glistening in the light of the oil lamp that hung in a wall bracket. She turned to face him, smiling. Her arms were dropped to her sides, and she spread them slightly as Longarm turned. The bosom-spots on her generous firm breasts were pebbled now, their tips extended, and the drops of water clinging to her dark pubic brush sparkled like small scattered diamonds.

For a moment Longarm stood both motionless and speechless. Then he found his voice and said, "Well, now. I sure got to give you credit for swapping looks fair and square."

"It won't be exactly fair until you drop your underwear," she replied.

Longarm's moments of surprise had passed now. He wasted no time in unbuttoning his long johns and pushing them down his legs to step out of them.

"Oh, my!" she exclaimed as he stepped up to the tub and she got her first clear view of his jutting erection. "I hadn't expected—" She stopped for a moment, then went on. "I hope you locked that door when you closed it a minute ago. Those people in the hall—"

"I locked it, so we ain't got a thing to worry about," he said, stepping into the tub.

"Then let's don't waste any time!" she said urgently.

As she spoke she was clasping her arms around Longarm's neck, her forearms resting on his broad shoulders. She levered herself upward, spreading her legs. Longarm placed himself quickly. She locked her legs around his hips, and as she tightened her thigh muscles to draw him into her, Longarm lunged.

A small scream of delight broke from her lips and she pressed her face on Longarm's shoulder to smother the sharp sudden sound. Her hips were twisting now, and Longarm felt the pressure of her heels on his back as she tried to pull him closer and draw him into her even more deeply.

"You just hang on," he said. "I'll do the rest."

Cradling her hips in his big strong hands, Longarm started the woman's body swaying back and forth. He found a steady rhythm and maintained it in spite of her squirming, drawing her to him with easy rhythmic tugs,

142

then swinging her backward before clasping her firmly and pulling her to him again while he lunged forward with his hips.

After a few moments, she began to squirm, twisting her hips as best she could in Longarm's hand-cradle, grasping his biceps and lifting herself enough to give her control of the increasingly frantic movements of her body. Longarm helped her as best he could, slowing his drives now, but still thrusting steadily as he maintained his rhythmic penetrations.

Suddenly he felt her body stiffen, a signal that her climax was not far off. Longarm slowed his lunges even more, but their longer duration only added intensity to the gyrations of her hips. Then she began gasping. She tensed her arms to lever herself a bit higher, and the rotation of her hips as she pulled Longarm into her now became a rolling wriggling squirming. The rolls of her hips were almost constant now and mounting in their intensity. A scream burst from her throat. She tried to smother it, but failed. Her movements were no longer controlled, but frantic.

Longarm knew that her climax was beginning, and lunged as deeply and as quickly as he could. When her final broken keening cries began, he clasped his hands more firmly and speeded his lunges to reach his own peak. A keening sob broke from her throat and her back arched as she twisted her hips faster. Longarm was ready. He thrust fiercely, matching her intensity now as he felt his own fulfillment approaching.

At last she loosed a final grating scream and her body tensed. The rhythmic undulation and twisting of her hips became spasmic, uncontrollable for several moments.

Only then did Longarm release his own long-pent-up urge. He thrust in a final deep lunge and held her closely to him while he jetted. She gasped for breath as her spasm ended and suddenly the strength seemed to leave her body.

Longarm held her while she quivered through the aftermath of her climax. He recovered control of his muscles more readily than she did, and began to breathe normally while she was still limp and gasping. Then she loosed a final sigh of satisfaction and turned her limpid eyes up to gaze at him.

"I did not intend this to happen," she said. "But I am not sorry that it did."

"I ain't sorry either, even if I didn't have no idea except getting a bath when I come in here."

While they were talking she twisted her shoulders in a tentative movement, and Longarm lowered her to her feet. She took a towel from the rack beside the tub and began rubbing his chest and shoulders dry.

"We should not stay here too long," she said as she rubbed the towel over his chest and the corded muscles of his stomach. "Others may be coming to bathe. My room is just across the hall, if it is empty of people now."

"Mine's next to yours, then, I guess," he told her. He stepped to the door and cracked it open to flick his eyes along the corridor. "There ain't nobody out there to see us, but I'd sooner tag along with you, if you ain't got any objection."

"I was getting ready to invite you," she said with a smile. "Let us gather up such clothing as we have and go where we will not be interrupted."

"Well, I'll sure be glad to go along with you. But we

better shake a leg and get outa here before somebody shows up."

Moving quickly, they gathered up the garments that had fallen to the floor. Without dressing, but after opening the door an inch or so to make another precautionary inspection of the corridor, they dashed quickly across it to her room.

"Perhaps we should introduce ourselves," she suggested as she turned the key in the door of her room. "I am Carlotta Isabella Solar de Pedernales, of the Rancho Palomar. It is in the Cumbres de Majalco, north of Chihuahua City."

"My name's Long, Custis Long," Longarm replied. "But mostly the folks I know best call me Longarm."

"Then after our pleasure in the bathtub, I feel that I know you well enough to do so too." She smiled. "Tell me, Longarm, do you have an occupation?"

"Oh, sure. I'm a deputy United States marshal outa the Denver office and I got sent here to take back a prisoner that's going on trail up there."

"But you are more than that," Carlotta went on. "You are a lover such as I have never known before."

"Well, Carlotta, I take that as a real nice compliment, if that's what you intended it to be."

"A compliment, yes. And an invitation. The night is yet young. Would you not like to spend it with me?"

Chapter 12

Feeling refreshed in spite of his lack of sleep the night just past, Longarm reined in at the entrance to *rurale* headquarters and dismounted. He secured the reins of the livery horse to the hitch rail. The led horse hitched by a length of rope to the saddlehorn of the one Longarm had been riding seemed secure enough, and he let it stand.

Taking the short flight of low steps two at a time, he went into the building. The long corridor beyond the entranceway was lined with doors. It was also totally deserted, and none of the opaque glass panes that formed the upper panels of the unbroken line of doors bore signs or inscriptions to identify them. Longarm smiled wryly as the thought occurred to him that he might well be in the Federal Building in Denver, heading for the marshal's office. Selecting one of the doors at random, he rapped on its glass panel.

"*Vente 'ca!*" a man's voice called from inside.

Longarm opened the door and stepped through it. The room he'd entered must have been devoted to files or archives, for beyond the counter that stretched its full width there were shelves piled to overflowing with stacks of paper. A youngish man was coming toward him from the far end of the room. He wore street garb, which was not unusual since the *rurales* had no standard uniforms.

"*Bueno dias, señor*," he said. "*Que queries?*"

"My name's Long, deputy United States Marshal," Longarm replied. "And I'm looking for one of your *rurales* named Carlos. Funny thing, I been riding with him a pretty good spell, and I never did even find out what his last name is."

"Ees only one Carlos een duty here," the clerk replied.

"If he's the only one, then he's got to be the man I'm looking for," Longarm told the man. "Now, if you'll just point out which one of these doors—"

"Ees better I show," the *rurale* broke in.

Longarm followed the clerk almost to the end of the long hallway, where the man stopped in front of a door which bore no identifying legend. His guide rapped twice, sharply. A moment passed before the door opened and Carlos stepped into the corridor. On seeing Longarm, he gestured for the clerk to leave, and as the man turned away Carlos said, "Come een, Longarm."

Longarm glanced around the small office. It was furnished with only a table and four or five chairs. A stack of papers, scrambled and scattered, covered the top of the table. Otherwise, the room was bare. Carlos waved toward one of the chairs and Longarm settled into it.

"This looks like quite some layout you got here," he said. "It sorta reminds me of the office I work out of in Denver."

"Eet ees not finish," Carlos told him, drawing up a

148

chair and settling into it across the table from Longarm. "Ees always sometheeng else to do."

"Sure," Longarm agreed. "And I don't aim to waste none of your time. All I come for is that Thad Miller rascal. I want to get him back to Denver soon as I can."

For a long moment Carlos did not reply, then he said, "I do not like to e-tell you thees, *amigo*. You have travel a long way, and eet weel not please you to go back weeth the hands empty, as you e-say een Los Estados Unidos. Bot I have the order from my *comandante* that we are not to sorrender to you thees Thad Meeller. He ees too much want here by Mexico."

"Now, wait just a damn minute!" Longarm exclaimed. "I traveled one hell of a lot of miles to get that son of a bitch, and I sure ain't going back across the border without him!"

Carlos shook his head as he said, "I have the fear that thees es what you most do, Longarm. And I speek as *amigo* een truth."

Though Longarm could sense the genuine regret in Carlos's voice, the *rurale*'s tone was firm.

Carlos went on. "Een Los Estados Unidos thees Miller ees want for much long time, so much I am know. *Tambien*, he ees want here too. He ees *asisieno, ladron, bastardo*."

"Now wait just a damn minute!" Longarm broke in when Carlos paused for breath. His was voice level but firm, "I ain't arguin' what he is or ain't. But the way I see it, he's an escaped prisoner that I have taken, and that means he belongs to us U.S. marshals."

"Are you forget I am weeth you when he ees recapture?" Carlos asked quickly.

"No," Longarm snapped. "And I ain't forgetting how much help you was either. But damn it, Carlos, he was already in our El Paso holdover a long time before he got away and went to take cover on the Island! And you know just as well as I do that the Island don't belong to your country any more'n it does to mine!"

"Thees does not deeference make! For the crimes een our country he moost be try!"

"As far as I can see, he'll get tried and get a hanging judgment. And he'll be just as dead if he's tried on the American side of the border as he'd be here in Mexico!"

"No!" Carlos rose to his feet. "Remeember, Longarm! Eef I do not help you on the Island, maybeso you do not go away from eet alive!"

"I ain't forgot that, and I owe you for it. But if I recall, I helped you a few times too, so that sorta evens things out. Now—" Longarm stopped short as a tattoo of knocks sounded on the door.

"*Entrase!*" Carlos called.

There was little hint of the *rurale* about the man who opened the door and stepped into the small room. He wore the loosely fitting pullover blouse and baggy trousers that were common to the laboring class, and a three- or four-day growth of beard straggled over his cheeks and chin. He was frowning, an expression not so much of puzzlement as of worry.

"What ees it you want, Chaco?" Carlos asked.

"*El capitan dime que contarte esta cosa,*" the newcomer replied. "*El prisionero Meeler, no 'sta en la celda.*"

Longarm's knowledge of Spanish was not great, but it was enough to allow him to understand what the man was saying. Even if he had not caught Thad Miller's name, the expression of shock which swept over Carlos's face and almost instantly became an angry frown was enough to translate the messenger's words.

Carlos was on his feet a few seconds sooner than Longarm. As he leaped from his chair he asked, "*Cuando?*"

Shrugging, the messenger replied, "*Nadies conocen.*"

Before Carlos could speak again, Longarm asked him, "Did I hear right, Carlos? Thad Miller's got away from your jail here, and nobody's got out after him yet?"

"So eet would seem," Carlos nodded. He turned back to the man in the doorway and asked, "*Como pelvorosa?*"

Again the messenger shrugged as he replied, "*Ninguno sabes. Solamente conocen que el prisionero desparece.*"

Carlos glanced questioningly at Longarm, who said, "I got enough to Spanish to pick up most of what he just said, and I can guess about the rest. I'd imagine that nobody knows how or when the son of a bitch got outa the cell he was in or where he might've took off to go. Is that close enough?"

Carlos nodded, then for a moment he stood silently thoughtful before replying. "I theenk you understan' enough of our language to have learn as much about thees as now myself I know."

"I reckon I missed a word or two, but I got the idea, all right," Longarm told him. He kept his anger in check, but could not keep from adding, "I'd say you got a damned big hole someplace in this jail of yours."

"Always ees somebody who does not do hees job right, Longarm," Carlos agreed. "Bot weethout he get a horse, Meeler weel not go far."

151

"How hard you think it's going to be for him to steal one?" Longarm asked. "Why, right this minute he might be in the saddle of a horse he's rustled, cutting a shuck for someplace that he's holed up in before, or maybe he's got someplace picked out that he found when he was on the run and seen it'd make him a good hidey-hole."

"Thees I am think of too, Longarm," Carlos said. "We weel send men out een all direction. Weel you do the same weeth the *mariscales federales* on your side from the reever?"

Remembering the chaotic condition of the U.S. marshal's office in El Paso during his earlier stop there, Longarm did not reply at once. A frown had formed on Carlos's face while he was waiting for an answer to his question. It did not vanish when Longarm's reply came.

"I guess you know I can't just go into the El Paso office and give orders to the chief marshal, Carlos," he said slowly. "Was I to start ordering his deputies around, he'd likely tell me to go jump in the Rio Grande. He's a new man on the job and it's likely he'd be pretty persnickety about the standing order that says we ain't supposed to go outside of U.S. territory."

"But you are een Mexico wheen we first meet, Longarm," Carlos said.

"Sure. But my boss is in Denver, and he knows when to look the other way if it comes down to one of us following a crook we're after. He don't go by the rule book the way a new chief marshal feels like he's got to."

"But you do not theenk the *jefe* een El Paso weel refuse to help you?"

"Now, that's hard to say," Longarm answered. "I disremember whether I told you this before now, but things in that office wasn't in the kinda shape they oughta be when I stopped in for a minute or so on my way here before I headed for the Island."

"Surely you do not theenk they weel refuse you!"

"Why, I just ain't going to give 'em a chance to turn me down, Carlos. Like I told you, I'll do the best I can, sure as God made little green apples."

"We weel need help from your side on the border to catch thees one," Carlos noted. "Meeler, he is bad like hees father. Ees queek weeth gun, very smart, very mean."

"You think he's crossed the Rio Grande, or is likely to?" Longarm frowned. "I got a hunch he'd stay in Mexico, because he knows what's waiting for him on the American side."

"Wheech ees only the esame theeng that ees wait for heem here in Mexico. Bot we cannot waste the time, Longarm. I most go at once."

"I don't reckon you'd mind if I was to tag along with you," Longarm said. "Seeing as we still ain't decided whether the son of a bitch belongs to your *rurales* or to our outfit."

"Thees we weel settle wheen we catch heem," Carlos said. "Bot eef you weel wait—"

"Don't bother about me, Carlos," Longarm replied quickly. "I know just what you're up against, and I'm smart enough to know this is your part of the country, not mine."

"I am glad you onderstand," Carlos nodded.

"I ain't finished yet," Longarm said. "I don't always play hunches, but this time I got a right smart mind to.

153

You want to hear about it, or is what you got to do so all-fired important that you figure you got to keep on with your job?"

For a moment Carlos was silently thoughtful, then he shrugged and said, "Eet ees my job I must do. Theen we weel talk of what you are e-theenk."

Longarm nodded as he replied, "I ain't going to argufy with you, Carlos. You got your way of doing things and I got mine. So I'm going to give you fair notice. If you and your outfit catches up with Thad Miller, I aim to get him away from you and haul him over the river to El Paso by any kind of hook or crook I can figure out."

A frown had been forming on Carlos's face while Longarm was talking. Now he said, "And I weel esay to you what you esay to me. Eef you are capture heem een Mexico, I weel take heem from you and keep heem here eef I can so do."

"I reckon we ain't got much else to say, then," Longarm told the *rurale*. Standing up, he went on. "I'll be starting out soon as I can get back to the hotel and pick up my saddlebags and rifle. I didn't figure I'd be starting back with that Miller fellow till after you and me done a little talking."

"We onderstan' each other," Carlos said. "Who ees take heem, they weel keep heem."

"And I don't figure it'll make much difference. Whether you and your *rurales* get him, or I do, he'll wind up swinging on the end of a rope."

"A rope eef you get heem, Longarm," Carlos said. "Eef we of the *rurales* do, he weel against the wall stand to be eshoot by firing squad. Bot he weel be just as dead, whichever way."

154

"I reckon it'll be no holds barred between us," Long-arm went on, "Just the Devil take the hindmost. But I figure we're both man enough to shake hands on it."

Longarm extended his hand as he was speaking and Carlos gripped it. Then without speaking again, Longarm turned and left the office. Reaching his horse, he mounted and rode back to El Pajaro Azul to pick up his rifle and saddlebags. He left the animal standing at the hitch rail in front of the hotel while he was inside.

After stopping at the desk long enough to settle his bill for his overnight stay, Longarm went upstairs to his room to pick up his saddlebags and rifle. He unlocked the door and stepped inside. His jaw dropped with surprise as he turned away from the door after stepping into the room and saw Carlotta stretched out on his bed. She was nude, her dressing gown in a huddle on the floor beside the bed. Her eyes were turned toward him and her full red lips were curled in a smile of anticipation.

"Carlotta!" Longarm exclaimed before she could speak. "I sure wasn't looking to find you in my room here!"

"And I was not sure you would come to mine again before you left," she replied. "The longer I thought of you the greater my wish grew to be with you again. As they say in your country, I have taken the bull by the horns. But you know why I have come here, I hope to take again the big horn you pleased me with so beautifully last night."

"Now, wait a minute!" Longarm protested. "I got to admit that I been thinking about you right regular since I left the hotel a little while ago. But I'm down here in Mexico on official business, Carlotta! I got to start out right away and try to run down a killer that got outa jail last night by some kind of hook or crook."

"And you have no time for me before you leave?"

Longarm hesitated for only a moment, in spite of the swelling that had begun in his groin. He tried not to think of the woman in his bed or to look at her too constantly, but whether he looked at her or away, he could not ignore with either his mind or his body the memory of the previous night and presence of the nude woman in his bed. Then duty edged out beauty and dictated his reply.

"I got my duty to think about," he said. "I swore my oath to do it, and I ain't one to go back on my word, Carlotta. I stand by what I say I'll do."

"I think all the better of you for saying that, Longarm," she told him. "But will you come back here when you capture this man you are after? If you are coming back, I will wait for you."

"Now, I guess that's one of the nicest things a woman can tell a man, Carlotta. But I can't make no promises, and I can't even make a guess when I might be back. I reckon all I can do is give you a good-bye kiss and hope we'll run into each other again later on."

Stepping up to the bed, Longarm bent down to reach Carlotta's lips. Her tongue darted out to seek his and as they held their kiss he felt her hands at his crotch, seeking the buttons of his trousers and freeing the erection that had begun with what he'd intended to be a chaste good-bye. Reluctantly, he broke the bond of their lips.

"Wait!" Carlotta said, her voice both urgent and pleading. "I must leave you with a memory that will bring you back to me, Longarm!"

Before he could reply or move to stop her, she slid an

arm around his hips to hold him in place and he felt her soft lips closing on him, engulfing him. Though Longarm knew he had little time to spare, he gave himself over to her caress.

All too soon, Carlotta's agile tongue and pulsing, clinging lips moving on his engorged shaft ended his effort to free himself. Longarm would have been less than human if he had used the force of his hands on her bobbing head to interrupt the mounting sensation of the expert worship she was expressing for his rigid shaft.

Carlotta did not hurry, and by the occasional spasmodic pulsations that shook her, Longarm realized that she was also responding to the pleasure she was bringing him. Each time she felt Longarm's body begin to quiver in the mounting response prompted by her caresses, Carlotta pushed her head forward to engulf him as deeply as possible. Her usually agile tongue flaccid and soft, she remained motionless, her questing tongue at rest, until Longarm's beginning shudders died away. Only then did she resume her soft caresses.

Minute after minute ticked away before Longarm reached the stage where he could no longer exercise the firmness of control that he'd been sustaining. Carlotta read Longarm's body-signals, and when at last she sensed that he could no longer restrain nature's inflexible demands, she carried him into the jerking jetting spasm of completion, holding him deeply while her face was pushed firmly into his pubic curls.

Looking up with her eyes opened wide as she drew away from him, Carlotta asked, "You will not forget me now, will you, Longarm?"

"There ain't a chance in the world that I'd ever be

able to," he assured her. "But I've just lost a prisoner who's taken me a long time to nab, and I got to start chasing him before he gets plumb outa reach."

"And of course you do not know where you must go, or when you will return."

"I just wish I did," Longarm said. "But if I could stay, I'd sure like to do just that. I ain't even sure that I'll be going through Juarez here when I start back."

"You will go where?"

"Like I said, I can't tell. And I might even cross the border someplace else, where it'd be easier for me to get to Denver in a hurry."

"Denver," Carlotta said thoughtfully. "I have never been to Denver. But I might enjoy visiting it, a bit later."

"Well, you'll know where to find me if you ever get there. "Longarm smiled. "Now, I got to go, Carlotta. Much as I'd like to stay, I got to put my duty first."

Bending for a farewell kiss, Longarm picked up his rifle and saddlebags and started for the door. He turned only long enough to wave a final good-bye as he left the room and started down the corridor toward the stairs.

"Well, now," Longarm said to Harris as the acting chief marshal of the El Paso office leaned back in his chair. "I guess we dotted all the i's and crossed the t's far as we can right now."

"I can't see anything we've missed, either," Harris agreed. "But I still say I can't see any reason for you thinking Miller might be trying to get away over Smuggler's Pass. My men have looked it over, and they wouldn't've missed anything."

"Oh, I ain't saying they did," Longarm told him. "Don't think I'm trying to be forward, and pushing my nose into your office's work, but if one of your deputies brings that Thad Miller in, I'd take it real kindly if you let me know real quick."

"I'm not trying to tell you how to handle your investigation, Long," Harris answered. "But hadn't you better tell me what your plans are?"

"Without meaning no disrespect to your badge, I don't talk about what I'm aiming to do. Not even to you. But I won't be gone more'n a day or two. I rented me a room over at the Del Norte Hotel, just so's I'd have a place here. If you come looking for me and I ain't in my room there, you just leave word. I ain't going to let that slippery son of a bitch get outa my sight once I got hold of him again."

"Don't worry, Long," Harris said. "I've got every man I can spare out looking for him. We're sure he's on our side of the Rio Grande now, and we're just as anxious to get rid of him as you are to have him."

"I'll be on my way, then," Longarm told Miller. "I got a hunch or two I want to play out, and if I'm right I'll likely be bringing Thad Miller back in handcuffs."

"Well, I wish you luck. My mind's going to rest a lot easier when I'm sure that you're on a train back to Denver and are taking that damned Miller with you."

"It'll ease my mind to get the cuffs on him too," Longarm said. "And the sooner I start, the sooner I'll be back, so I'll say good-bye now and be on my way."

Chapter 13

When he rode away from the marshal's office after his
talk with Doug Harris, Longarm reined his horse north.
He passed the area where the trim, well-kept houses that
lined the firm graveled road began to give way to shanties and hovels. The small ramshackle structures of the
area through which he was now riding had been cobbled
together from short lengths of boards and shingles and
rusted sheets of tin. Wide depressions that would become
potholes after one of the region's infrequent rains began
to appear in the street. Then suddenly the graveled road
ended.

Beyond the point Longarm had now reached the well-
tended street became a trail, and the houses no longer
stood in neat rows. The path meandered through a maze
of huts and shakedowns with cracked sagging doors and
glassless window openings. Here and there a tent had
been pitched among the more permanent dwellings. In
some spots the dwellings huddled together, in others
they were scattered at random and widely spaced. Some
were without doors and had slits in the walls instead of

window-openings. Occasionally Longarm got a momentary glimpse of the face of a child who was peering through one of the gaps.

Abruptly, the last traces of El Paso ended and the trail that started where the street ended wound ahead of him through open desert. Far beyond, barely visible through the shimmering heat-haze, he could now see the distant rounded hump of Sugarloaf Hill. Using it as his guide, for the trail was hard to follow on the barren hard-baked soil, Longarm kept his horse to a steady walk.

Though he was usually a patient man, there were moments as the horse veered from side to side on the unpredictably curved trail when Longarm was tempted to spur the animal to a gallop. He pushed the urge aside. The heat of the day had begun now, and though his mount was beginning to slow down, Longarm let it set its own gait, touching the reins only occasionally as it plodded along the trail that Longarm could now see was now beginning to wind across the gentle upslope.

As best Longarm could judge, Sugarloaf Hill was still a good hour's ride away, and the burning sun was nearly at its noon zenith when above and beyond the hill the tips of the low-rising Organ Mountains began to show on the northern horizon. They protruded above the elongated crest at the pass, dark rounded bulges like the tips of a panther's forepaws. Above them for a short distance a ghostly haze shimmered, veiling the blue distance beyond the crests and half hiding the jagged skyline.

On the path which Longarm continued to follow, the signs of travel diminished as he passed the spots where slits of canyons yawned. Now and then he came to places where smaller, less-used trails branched off the main one. In some areas where the hooves of horses and cattle had left scattered prints in the sandy soil, rock patches covered the ground and the trail almost disappeared.

At such places Longarm reined in to give himself a chance to study the trail markings more closely. Usually there were the hoofprints of cattle mixed with those of horse's hooves, and they often obliterated them on the side-branches that turned off from the main trail. A thin layer of soil generally covered the faintly marked path beyond the rock covered stretches, and Longarm gave these areas the same close attention that marked his inspection of the trail itself.

At some of the branches he dismounted and walked a short distance to explore the area on foot in order to give his horse a longer rest. Almost always the trail led to a canyon, and in most of these there was evidence of overnight camps. Some of the silent clues told him of even longer stays: dead ashes, horse and cattle droppings dried and crumbling, a spat-out wad of black long-dried chewing tobacco or the weathered, tattered butt of a cigar or cigarette.

Though Longarm was generally a patient man, there were moments when he looked ahead at the long rise and felt a sudden impulse to spur his mount to a gallop instead of allowing it to set its own pace up the long gentle slope. The feeling passed quickly, for the horse was moving even more reluctantly now. After Longarm had dismounted and gone to explore one of its better-marked branches for a short distance, zigzagging across the area,

163

he returned to his horse and stood for a moment beside it as he studied the slope ahead.

"Now, look here, old son," he muttered. "You're acting like a plumb tenderfoot. It's about time you settled down to business or you'll be tromping all over hell's half-acre without doing nothing but wasting good shoe leather. Now, get back up on that nag and stop wasting good daylight."

None too soon to please Longarm, the dominating bulk of Sugarloaf Hill began to hide the furthest peaks, and against the clear blue sky he could see the hill's humped contours more clearly. In spite of the time that had passed since he'd closed the last case that brought him to the area, Longarm was able to recall the lay of the land ahead. When he'd gotten close enough to make out details of the base from which Sugarloaf Hill slanted upward, he reined in.

Slipping one of his long slim cigars out of his pocket, Longarm then fumbled a match from his vest pocket and rasped it with a thumbnail into a briefly flaring fizz, which soon settled to a steady flame. He touched the match to the tip of his cigar and sat studying Sugarloaf Hill's contours and creases. After a half-dozen thoughtful puffs, he nodded and waited for the blue filmy smoke to dissipate while he gave his full attention to the slope ahead.

"There ain't no way to be out-and-out certain, old son," he muttered when he'd taken his cigar from his lips. "But it's a safe bet there ain't enough rustled steers drove over this trail nowadays to wipe out horse tracks. And there sure ain't no big lot of horses' hoofprints, neither."

Once more Longarm toed his horse ahead. He watched the trail in front of him even more closely now, and at last he found the fresh hoof marks that he'd been seeking. Dismounting once more, he bent to get a closer view of the U-shaped impressions on the hoof-pocked stretch of beaten earth.

As he studied them, moving along the trail one slow step at a time, he came across a heap of horse dung. A glance told him it was fresh, and question grew to certainty. As he toed his horse up the wide winding trail to Sugarloaf Hill, he told himself thoughtfully, "If all the signs ain't lying, old son, you ain't got much longer to go. This trail's the one a man that didn't want to be noticed much would be most apt to take, so up to now it looks like your hunch might just be good."

Leading his horse, Longarm resumed his slow progress. There were fewer confusing hoofprints now, and he could see from those of the horse that had drawn his attention that it was favoring one of its hooves. More often than not in the stretches where the baked soil's hard crust gave way to sandier, softer dirt, the shallow prints of the animal's front hooves and the left rear hoof were clearly visible. They made deeper, fuller prints than did the arch of the right rear hoof.

"That'd figure," Longarm muttered around the stumpy butt of the cigar locked in his jaws. "Them damn big rocks is hell before breakfast on a bad-shod horse. Now, sure as God made little green apples them's the tracks of the nag Thad Miller stole when he got away, and from looking at them tracks even a half-blind man could tell the critter's gone lame. Which means Thad Miller can't be too far ahead. You know, old son, if all them new

165

deputies in that El Paso office had the brains God give a constipated jackass, they'd've beat you here for certain."

Looking ahead through the fringe of brush and stunted desert juniper trees, Longarm could tell by the steeper rise in the ground that he was nearing the rounded top of Sugarloaf Hill. Buoyed by the thought that he was now very close to his objective, he started scanning the path more closely than ever. He'd mounted the hump of the hill, and was starting down on its other side before he saw the off-trail he'd been seeking.

"Now, that's more like it," he muttered.

Dismounting once again, he studied the off-trail. It was a barely visible trace on the hard tan soil. The only evidence that it had been disturbed recently was not in the baked earth. Longarm took his clues from a few badly bent stalks in a juniper bush beside the trail and two or three patches of small scrapes on the ground almost covered by the bent and broken plant stems in a thick clump of mixed grass and weeds.

Longarm led his horse off the trail now. He tethered it beyond the brush clump to one of the weathered jagged junipers where it would not be noticed from the road. He took his Winchester from its saddle scabbard and started zigzagging across the gentle hump of Sugarloaf Hill as he followed the barely discernible trail that he'd uncovered.

He moved even more slowly than before, making as little noise as possible, though to him the rustling of the grasses and patches of waist-high juniper shoots sounded loud indeed. Once when the brush crackled on one side of him, he turned and had his rifle leveled in the direction of the sound. Then he saw the fluffy white tail and dun-gray back-fur of a jackrabbit as it bounced through the undergrowth.

A bit sheepishly, Longarm lowered the Winchester. He reached into his pocket for a cigar. He had it in his mouth and was ready to light it before the need for caution cancelled habit. He suddenly realized that in the clear air atop the hump of Sugarloaf Hill, the scent of tobacco smoke carried by some vagrant wind would give the still-unsuspecting outlaw a signal as clear as the ringing of a gong. Replacing the cheroot in his vest pocket, he resumed his careful passage. From time to time as he moved forward he stopped to listen, but during none of his stops did he hear any sounds except the soft rustle of the light breeze through the brittle brush.

He'd covered perhaps a half mile when he caught the first scent of something burning. Though he saw no smoke, Longarm stopped at once and began a careful survey of the ground that sloped away from him on both sides of the gently arched crest. The day was well along now and the fitful breezes were dying.

During the time that Longarm had been making his slow advance he'd scanned the horizon ahead without glimpsing even a hint of rising smoke. He'd stopped and was swiveling his head slowly to view the horizon again while glancing only occasionally at the sky when he saw the faint, almost invisible shimmer of heat waves trembling in the clear air.

During the time that he'd been making his slow advance toward Thad Miller's hidey-hole, Longarm had been trying to come up with a plan that would allow him to capture Miller without having to shoot him. Now, with only half a plan to follow, he paused and glanced around, looking for a landmark that he could use to guide by as he left the trail in his slow advance through the featureless waist-high growth.

Longarm saw no landmarks he might use, but a few paces ahead there was a clump of juniper that towered a good foot or more above its surroundings. Stopping when he reached the tall wrist-thick trunks of the clump, Longarm reached as high as possible and locked both hands around the stalk of the tallest trunk within his reach. For several moments the tough pliant woody stalk resisted his efforts to snap it, but when he twisted the stalk while bending it between his locked fists, the juniper yielded.

Its green core-wood cracked softly, and Longarm pushed the top of the broken stalk firmly into the fork of a second tall upshoot that grew close to it. At a glance the slanting branch looked as though it had grown that way naturally. After a close look at his improvised guide, to be sure that the trail marker he'd created would deceive anyone but himself, Longarm nodded with satisfaction.

Picking up his rifle, he forged ahead. The heat ripples that had drawn his attention were closer now. Longarm continued his careful advance, and he'd gone only a short distance before he saw on the trail a brown lump of horse droppings, shining fresh.

"I guess that's about all you need to make sure you had a good hunch, old son," he said. "Them ain't more'n an hour old, if they're that much. Looks like it's time for you to move easy and keep your eyes wide open."

He'd covered only a hundred yards or so when he heard an occasional faint scraping of booted feet beyond the increasingly scant growth of weeds and an occasional juniper clump that still hid what lay ahead of him.

Now that he was close enough for his movements to be noticed by the outlaw, Longarm dropped belly-down and began an inch-by-inch forward crawl. His new posture made his progress even slower than his advance had been before, and now and again he glanced back at his marker to be sure that he was not veering off the course he'd chosen to follow. Though the grass patches were fewer and thinner, their stems had dried more thoroughly than those in more sheltered places. The brittle brush crackled under his weight and he began edging around them, just as he was forced to do when avoiding the roots of the juniper.

Telling himself that he was getting closer to Thad Miller with every inch his movements covered, Longarm ignored the small shoots of pain that stabbed his knees when he had to cross a stretch of ground thickly strewn with sharp pebbles. Pressing his lips together each time he encountered such patches, he kept up his slow advance.

Though the distance he covered seemed endless, Longarm had been at his squirming advance for only a few minutes when he began to see flickers of movement in the small spaces between the ground-hugging grass clumps and the drooping branches of the stunted juniper. He stopped when he got his first glimpse of a man's moving form. Flattening out, he lay rock-still, hidden by a shielding branch from one of the juniper bushes.

Longarm still could not make out any details of the movements of the outlaw. The ground growth concealed

Miller from him just as it was concealing him from Miller. Longarm did not try to resume his slow advance, but lay motionless for a moment while he tackled his next job: puzzling out the best way to capture Thad Miller without shooting him.

Chapter 14

Minutes ticked away. Longarm was well aware of the danger he was risking by delaying his final move, but he knew that when he did move on the killer for a show-down he had to have a workable plan that was within range of being executed with his limited resources. He must move to take Miller prisoner swiftly and without slipups.

Thad Miller was a killer, a man who'd shown himself to be as skillful with a gun and as merciless as his father had been. Longarm had no illusions about the fugitive being an easy man to capture alive.

He'd crept close enough to Miller now to see the outlaw's form, but only as a dark silhouetted hump lounging in the small cleared space that surrounded a long-dead campfire. The horse on which he'd escaped stood with its head down a few paces away.

Miller had not been foolhardy enough to give away his presence by lighting a campfire, but he was eating— exactly what, Longarm could not tell. Longarm saw that the renegade had managed to find a gunbelt somewhere, as well as a revolver. The small clearing in the screening brush where the outlaw had stopped was only a few dozen yards away, a dangerously short distance from the place Longarm had selected.

Longarm was too old a hand to risk letting himself be spotted by a fast-draw dead-shot gunman like Miller. He looked around, trying to find cover, a place where he could think out a line of attack that would allow him to keep his promise to Billy Vail and capture Miller without killing him.

On the rounded humped summit of Sugarloaf Hill Longarm could see very few resources. The best—in fact, the only—cover that he saw was a mixed stand of brushy juniper and thin grass. There was a boulder near the center of the sparse growth, and a cactus plant stood at its edge. Longarm settled down behind the thin screen of juniper to watch the outlaw and wait for the moment when the time was right to move against his quarry.

"Old son," he told himself silently, "that kind shoots when a lawman tells 'em to give up. The trouble is, if you was to shoot him and not give him a chance to lay his gun down peaceful, that'd be murder and you wouldn't be no better'n he is. Besides that, you gave Billy Vail your word you'd do just like he said and bring Thad Miller in alive, so you ain't got no druthers. What you better do is figure out real sudden how to keep that fool promise you made Billy."

As habit had led him to do when he was given time to plan before taking action, Longarm reached for one of the cigars in his vest pocket. He took the cheroot from his pocket in an automatic gesture, then shook his head at his thoughtless move, which would have given Miller

172

a target. He let the hand holding the cigar fall, and even before it came to rest on his thigh the possibilities of his position struck him.

Longarm had not moved into the position he occupied out of free choice. It was simply the only cover close to Miller on the hill's generally barren hump. In some respects it was as exposed as the little open patch chosen by Miller.

At each end of the spot where Longarm was stretched out behind the high round-topped rock, big juniper bushes grew a bit more than head-high. Their central stems were somewhat larger than a man's wrist, but their upthrust branches were no bigger than a thumb. A few patches of grass sprouted around the boulder, their faded green tendrils crawling along the surface of the arid soil. An arm's length away a cactus stood alone.

As he looked at the cigar he'd just taken from his mouth, a thoughtful frown formed on Longarm's face. After a moment passed he said in a half whisper, "Maybe you ain't got nobody to stand backup, old son, but it just might be you got something damn near as good. All you need to do is figure how to work things out, and that sure ain't going to take long."

For a moment, Longarm studied the ground around him. A fork in one of the junipers a few feet away seemed to fit his needs. Moving as silently as possible, he rolled over to it and began examining both the rock and the brush around it.

He saw at once that the juniper had grown up around the bottom of the boulder; its roots entered the earth below the big rock and forked just above the big rock's rounded top. On both sides of the juniper the tough pliant strings of grass covered the ground scantily. The lone cactus plant stood at the edge of the grassed area. Its long needle-sharp spines bristled thickly.

"Old son," Longarm told himself as he studied the scanty patch of vegetation, "it looks like you got just about all you need, soon as you dig a little bit more outa your pocket."

Laying his rifle aside, Longarm hunkered down by the boulder. He grabbed a double handful of the long grass tendrils out of the sandy soil, being careful to select the greenest and the strongest. Draping them over the big rock's gentle hump, he turned his attention to the juniper.

Though the branches he tested by pulling and flexing were thin, they were strong and springy. While he worked he returned the cigar to his mouth, but this time he did not reach for a match. Instead he began plaiting three long strands of the tough-skinned limber grass into a makeshift length of cord. Not all the tendrils were the same length, and when one of them proved too short, he lapped it in a twist to the one in place and continued his weaving until he had a strong grass string four or five feet long.

Now he went back to the juniper. He selected a branch with a fork in it, and with quick slashes of his pocketknife he cut off the ends above the fork until they were a bit more than an inch long. He whittled the other end to a sharp point, then set about making a twin to the fork he'd just finished. Longarm forced one of the forked sticks into the ground beside the boulder where it would be hidden from sight by the juniper's foliage.

Picking up his rifle, he sighted it on the form of the

sleeping outlaw as best he could through the brush. Keeping the stock steady to maintain the weapon's line of fire, he thrust the second forked stick into the ground below its buttstock.

He placed the Winchester's forestock into the V of the front stick and the butt in the notch of the second. Dropping to his knees, he made sure the rifle barrel was still aiming in the general direction of the spot where Thad Miller lay sleeping.

"Likely this won't put a bullet anyplace close to where that outlaw's at," Longarm muttered as he squinted along the barrel. "But if my luck holds it'll kick up some dust real close to him. But don't forget this next part's what's trickiest, old son."

Laying the rifle in the V's of the crotched juniper branches, Longarm took his thin cord of plaited grass and tied one end to the bottom of the nearest juniper bush. He doubled the string of grass into one strand and pulled back the rifle's hammer; then while holding the hammer in place with his thumb, he squeezed the trigger, knowing the gun would not fire until the hammer was released.

Hunkering back on his heels, Longarm wrapped several strands of plaited grass around the notch of the hammer to bind it to the stock. Then he braided the end of the grass string back to the juniper bush by twisting it a half-dozen times, and tied the end off on the juniper branch above the knot that secured the second string.

Finally, Longarm lighted the cigar he'd been holding in his jaws. He puffed it furiously for a moment, squinting to study the length of the red coal glowing at the tip of the long thin cheroot. He gauged the speed at which the ash formed on the tip of the cigar as the lighted tip glowed.

When he was satisfied that he had a good idea of its timing, he lashed the cigar at right angles to the grass-string which secured the trigger and held it to its guard. Then Longarm strung the end of the grass cord to the length of string stretched to the juniper. The glowing cigar dangled in midair, suspended midway between the rifle and the juniper bush.

Now Longarm removed the shell that was in the rifle's chamber and pulled the hammer back to full cock. He held his thumb tightly on the hammer while he pulled the trigger, and placed the rifle in the rest he'd made. With his free hand he wound several turns of the grass cord in the notch of the hammer and around the throat of the stock to hold the hammer in the full-cock position.

Gingerly, Longarm released the hammer from the pressure of his thumb. When it strained against the loops of the improvised grass cord but did not snap into the firing slot, Longarm loosed a sigh of relief. Lifting the rifle, careful not to disturb the grass-cord lashing, he broke the rifle to slide a shell into the chamber and snapped the action shut.

He exhaled another deep breath when the tension of the hammer's firing spring failed for the second time to snap the flimsy improvised lashing, but stayed at full cock. Bending down, he secured the cigar firmly to the grass string. He adjusted the glowing end to a length that would give him time to move into position across the trail. As a final bit of insurance that his scheme would work, Longarm puffed at the cigar until the coal at its tip was bright red while he studied the length of the ash that extended beyond the glowing tip.

Standing up, Longarm gave a last glance at the contrivance he'd created. It had at least a chance of working. Then he started for Thad Miller's hiding-place on the other side of the trail. He moved steadily, as silently as possible, though the grating of his boot soles on the raw arid earth when he crossed the trail sounded loud to him.

Dividing his attention between keeping his eyes on the ground ahead and flicking them toward the small coulee where he'd last seen the escaped outlaw, Longarm picked his way carefully across the trail to the edge of the little clearing by the coulee. Though it seemed that hours passed while he covered the short distance, Longarm knew that he still had enough time.

He circled the little coulee where he'd seen Miller, and from then on advanced even more slowly than before. When at last he glimpsed Miller, the escaped outlaw was still stretched out, his hands clasped behind his head, gazing at the bright sky. Longarm edged as close as he dared to the rim of the little depression, and dropped to one knee. He drew his revolver as he waited.

Longarm's wait was not a long one. Miller had not moved since the last time Longarm had sighted him. He was still stretched out on the ground, his hands clasped behind his head, his eyes closed.

When the burning cigar across the trail touched the strands of grass that were holding down the hammer of Longarm's rifle, the freed hammer snapped down on the rifle's firing pin. The report of the shot and the rifle slug whistling above his head brought Miller to his feet. He

177

whipped out his revolver as he rose and dropped into a gunfighter's crouch, facing the direction from which the shot had come.

Longarm let off his own shot now. The slug thunked into the ground between the gunfighter's feet. Before Miller could swivel around, Longarm called, "Drop the gun and put up your hands, Miller! You ain't got a chance!"

For a fraction of a second Longarm thought that he was going to be forced to break his promise to Billy Vail that he would bring Thad Miller to Denver alive. The gunman hesitated only a moment, then let his pistol drop to the ground.

"Now, step away from the gun!" Longarm commanded.

Again, Miller obeyed. Keeping his eyes fixed on his quarry, Longarm stepped close enough to kick the gun out of Miller's reach. The gunfighter turned his head, sheer hatred glowing in his obsidian eyes.

Longarm returned the stare, his eyes as cold as Miller's. He said, "Now take off your gunbelt and your pants-belt, too."

"Why the hell should I?" Miller snarled.

"Because I'm telling you to!" Longarm snapped. "If you got a derringer in back of your belt buckle, I don't aim to give you a chance to use it."

For a moment Miller hesitated, and Longarm stepped up to him close enough to jab the Colt's muzzle against his backbone. His hands moving slowly, the outlaw unbuckled his gunbelt and let it drop to the ground. Even more reluctantly he took off the belt that supported his trousers and let it fall also. Almost at once, his breeches began sliding down his thighs and stopped as they bundled below his knees, trapping his feet.

"Now I ain't going to be worried so much about you running away," Longarm told him. "Was you to luck out, there ain't many places a man can go without he's got pants on. Now put your hands in back of you. You're such a slippery son of a bitch that I don't aim to give you no chance for tricks."

After Longarm had pulled Miller's wrists behind him and snapped on his handcuffs, he went on. "My horse is a little ways off. You go first and I'll keep my Colt jabbed into your backbone and lead your horse till we get to mine."

Miller remained sullenly silent and stood motionless. Longarm prodded him with the muzzle of his revolver. As he stepped away from his huddled trousers, the outlaw protested, "Ain't you going to let me wear my pants to wherever we're going?"

"You ain't going to be no better-looking with your britches on than you are with 'em off," Longarm grunted. "But I ain't one to shame a man by prodding him into town half-dressed. I'll toss 'em over my shoulder and you can put 'em on before we start to town."

Scooping up Miller's pants, Longarm tossed them over his shoulder. The heavy wide tooled belt slipped from its loops and dropped to the ground.

"Hey, I need that belt!" Miller said quickly.

Keeping his eyes on Miller, Longarm hunkered down and groped for the belt. As he slid his fingers along its inner surface they encountered an odd bulged spot. Longarm looked at the lining and saw that it had been split. He squeezed the slit open and saw two keys shining

179

in the little hidden cache. Thumbing the keys from the slit, he examined them. One was a tiny handcuff key, the second a long flat key of the type used in the locks of jail cells.

"Well, just look at what you got here!" Longarm said. "Handcuff key and jail-cell key. No wonder you been able to get away from the law and bust outa jail so easy! I'll give you the belt and just keep the keys. You get into your britches as fast as you can. We got a train to catch when we get back to El Paso, and you got a date with a judge that'll likely wind up with you taking the thirteen gallows steps. Now, march!"

A *special offer for people who enjoy reading the best Westerns published today. If you enjoyed this book, subscribe now and get . . .*

TWO FREE

A $5.90 VALUE—NO OBLIGATION

If you enjoyed this book and would like to read more of the very best Westerns being published today, you'll want to subscribe to True Value's Western Home Subscription Service. If you enjoyed the book you just read and want more of the most exciting, adventurous, action packed Westerns, subscribe now.

Each month the editors of True Value will select the 6 very best Westerns from America's leading publishers for special readers like you. You'll be able to preview these new titles as soon as they are published, FREE for ten days with no obligation.

TWO FREE BOOKS

When you subscribe, we'll send you your first month's shipment of the newest and best 6 Westerns for you to preview. With your first shipment, two of these books will be yours as our introductory gift to you absolutely FREE, regardless of what you decide to do. If you like them, as much as we think you will, keep all six books but pay for just 4 at the low subscriber rate of just $2.45 each. If you decide to return them, keep 2 of the titles as our gift. No obligation.

Special Subscriber Savings

When you become a True Value subscriber you'll save money several ways. First, all regular monthly selections will be billed at the low subscriber price of just $2.45 each. That's

WESTERNS!

at least a savings of $3.00 each month below the publishers price. Second, there is never any shipping, handling or other hidden charges—Free home delivery. What's more there is no minimum number of books you must buy, you may return any selection for full credit and you can cancel your subscription at any time. A TRUE VALUE!

Mail the coupon below

To start your subscription and receive 2 FREE WESTERNS, fill out the coupon below and mail it today. We'll send your first shipment which includes 2 FREE BOOKS as soon as we receive it.